Timeless

G.W. Mullins

Light Of The Moon Publishing

ISBN: 978-1-64871-177-0

First Edition Printing

This is a work of fiction. Names, characters, businesses, places, events and incidents are either the products of the author's imagination or used in a fictitious manner. Any resemblance to actual persons, living or dead, or actual events is purely coincidental.

Light Of The Moon Publishing has allowed this work to remain exactly as the author intended, verbatim, without editorial input.

Printed in the United States of America

For further information, on the writing, visit G.W. Mullins' web site at http://gwmullins.wix.com/books

Also Available from G.W. Mullins In Hardback, Paperback and eBook

Rise Of The Dark-Lighter Book One: Dark Awakening

From the Author of the Best-Selling Book Series "From The Dead Of Night"

Rise of the Darklighter

Book One

Dark Awakening

To fight evil, you have to embrace the darkness

G. W. Mullins

In order to save his uncle, Malachi is forced to summon Santa Muerte, the deity of death. He offers a year of his life in exchange for her help. With his soul on the line, he must do her bidding, to regain his freedom.

He quickly learns a battle is about to begin. The dead begin to rise, as Angels and Demons prepare to wage war for control of humanity. Empowered as a Dark-Lighter, Malachi must choose a side as Armageddon begins to take place, and the last battle between good and evil begins.

"Dark Awakening" is the first of three books from Author G.W. Mullins' "Rise Of The Dark Lighter." This new series is a continuation of his "From The Dead Of Night" books, featuring the Best-Selling titles "Daniel Is Waiting" and "Daniel Returns."

***Rise Of The
Snow Queen
Book Two:
The War Of The Witches***

What begins as a simple, bittersweet tale about a man turned into a polar bear, grandly unfolds into a rich, mythical adventure in the best-selling book series Rise Of The Snow Queen. Based on Hans Christian Andersen's

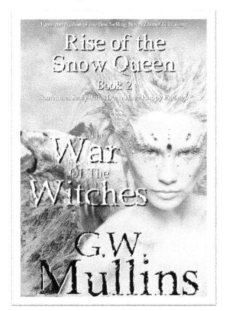

fairy tale, author G.W. Mullins expands on this story creating a new mythology that takes readers into the world of snow and ice.

In part two, the story develops long before the adventures of Gerda and Kai. It takes readers to a remote mountain village where winter claims lives at the Snow Queen's command. The story goes back to the Mirror and how it cracked, sending its shards into the world to infect the innocent. This take on the story, embarks on a much more adult tone with the mood turning rather sinister as the Snow Queen battles to obtain the mirror and rule them all. Rise Of The Snow Queen Two - War Of The Witches, is a dark fairy tale that unfolds to a conclusion you won't expect to see coming.

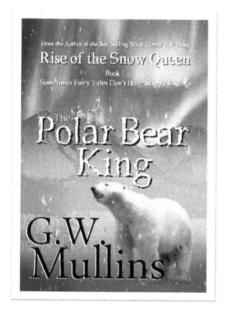

Rise Of The Snow Queen Book One: The Polar Bear King

The first book from the new "Rise Of The Snow Queen" four part series.

G.W. Mullins has taken timeless folklore and crafted it into a new book series meant for adults. His updated take on the Polar Bear King and Snow Queen pay homage to the stories we all loved as

children while making them more adventurous and not always allowing for a "happily ever after" ending.
The newly crowned King Valeman refuses to marry an evil witch, who reveals herself to be the infamous Snow Queen. His refusal to align himself with the dark forces causes her to cast an enchantment upon him.

Her unbreakable spell changes him beyond belief. "By light one way, by night another. Your form will change you will soon discover. By day a beast of a bear you will be, at night a man while others sleep. To break this spell you much achieve, the love of another while being a beast."

Valeman is transformed into the Polar Bear King and given seven years to find true love or the enchantment will be permanent.

Daniel Awakens
A Ghost Story Begins

Death Is Only The
Beginning

Author G.W. Mullins
turns back time in his
Best-Selling "From The
Dead Of Night" book
series.

In Daniel Awakens A
Ghost Story Begins,
Mullins takes you back
to the day Daniel died.
In a welcome addition
to the fan favorite series, readers will learn what happened
to Daniel.

Daniel had known his whole life something was not right.
He never connected with the woman who he was told was
his mother. As his sixteenth birthday approached, he
learned the life he had lived was based around a hidden
past. His worst suspicions were realized when the truth of
his father's affair came to light. As Daniel ran from the
house of lies, he had no idea his young life was about to
end.

Daniel awakened in the cemetery, and quickly came to
learn death is only the beginning. Thrust into a world of

the undead, he had no time to learn of the afterlife or the battle of good and evil. The dark ones were coming, whether he was ready or not, he would soon learn of the dark-lighters and a force of evil named Malachi.

Destined to be a leader in the fight for the balance of power, Daniel is thrust into a battle he is not ready for. He quickly learns of his abilities and the lack of experience he has to control them. Daniel must fight to save the force of good.

Daniel's Fate
A Ghost Story Ends
"From the Dead Of
Night" Book Four

Daniel walked in the
land of the
Dead. Now the Dead
want him back.

As the dark ones came for Daniel, he was forced to take refuge in the light, the last place he wanted to be. There, he was to

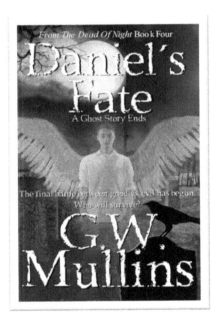

decide his own fate. Staying in the light and ascending meant

Jen would be left defenseless. If he chose being human again, the dark ones would have the

power to take over the world. As Daniel made his decision, the dead began to rise. The dark

ones were coming forward to block the light and create hell on earth.

Death is only the beginning... From The Dead Of Night Book 4

***Daniel Is Waiting
A Ghost Story
"From the Dead Of
Night" Book One***

***Daniel walked in the
land of the dead. Now
the dead want him
back!***

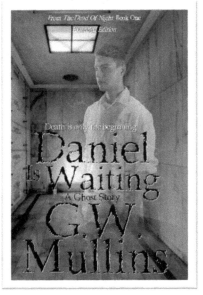

The veil is lifted
between the living and
the dead as the
Shadows come forward
to capture him.

Daniel Stratton died in
a tragic accident. His life should have been over but it was
not. His spirit spent the next sixty years trying to
communicate with the people who came to the cemetery
where he was entombed. Then Jen came one night to the
mausoleum seeking refuge from a life that was spinning out
of control. There she found Daniel.

As they work together to free him from his forced
confinement; they learn that the Light comes for all dead,
and Daniel is forced to enter it. In his case there is no
matter of choice. Inside he fights for his life and escapes
but the enforcers of the light come for him. He saw seven
of these shadow people within the light and each marked

him. Daniel knows these Shadows will come for him. Each one of the seven will take the body of a human who had just succumbed to death turning them to Zombie like creatures to do their bidding.

Together Daniel and Jen must confront the "Shadows" so that they can survive to see another day.

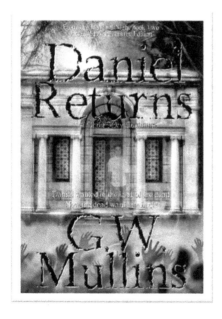

Daniel Returns A Ghost Story "From The Dead Of Night" Book Two

Daniel walked in the land of the dead. Now the dead want him back!

The story continues where "Daniel Is Waiting A Ghost Story" ended in a cliff hanger.

Daniel died a tragic death and should be dead. He walked in the land of the dead for too long. Then the light came for him but he refused it. He fought to escape it, but higher powers had other plans for him.

His fate was to ascend and take on the role of angel, but something went wrong. Before he could assume his role, he met Jen. When Daniel fought the light to stay with Jen, he broke the law of the dead. Within the light seven Shadow enforcers saw him. They reached out to stop him and in doing so marked him. When Daniel escaped, he knew the seven would come for him.

The forces of good and evil watch to see who can claim Daniel in the end and control the ultimate power that is growing within him.

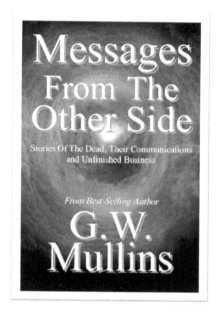

Messages From The Other Side Stories of the Dead, Their Communication, and Unfinished Business

Best-selling author G.W. Mullins shares his personal journey towards understanding death, the afterlife and communication with spirits of loved ones who have passed over. In "Messages From The Other Side Stories of the Dead, Their Communication, and Unfinished Business," Mullins tells of dealing with the grief of his mother passing and the reassurance of an after death communication that totally changed his outlook towards death and grief.

This book not only tells of Mullins' personal journey into understanding but also guides others to understand why we receive communications and the signs to look for. Mullins also explores visitation dreams and tells of his own personal experience in the area and shares the stories of others who have had similar experiences.

This book highlights the author's personal journey in an exploration for knowledge, and his understanding, without question, there is life after death. Mullins invites you to join him on this journey through life and death.

Vengeance
A Paranormal
Murder Mystery

"Mystery, Murder, Paranormal Events, and a story that leaves you guessing as the bodies stack up."
– Matthew Trent
OutLoud Magazine

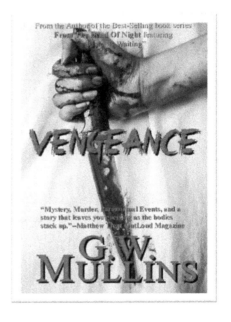

After the death of her father, Danni starts a new life in a seaside town in New York where she and her mother move into a strange Gothic house with a terrible history. From the moment Danni gets there, she feels she is being watched. She is sure they are not alone in the house.

As Danni learns of her new home, she is told of a past resident who fell to her death on the nearby cliffs at the same time that her teenaged daughter, Elizabeth, disappeared.

Elizabeth's spirit, appears to Danni and claims that her mother's death was a murder, not suicide and asks for Danni's help in bringing the dangerous killer to justice.

The mystery unfolds as Danni enlists the help of the hunky new friend she has made named Joe. A romance develops between them, but does Joe know more about the murder and disappearance than he is letting on? Will Danni live to solve the murder?

Other titles available from G.W. Mullins include:

The Native American Story Book Volume 1-5- Stories Of The American Indians For Children

Walking With Spirits Volumes 1-6 Native American Myths, Legends, And Folklore

The Native American Cookbook

Star People, Sky Gods And Other Tales of The Native American Indians

Cherokee A Collection of American Indian Legends, Stories And Fables

For Clarence

Prologue

Inside the barn the two lovers were beginning what would be their last fight. Stephanie never understood how Chance could fly into jealous rages the way he did. But that night he was more out of control than ever. Stephanie pleaded with him to hear the truth, but he would have no part of it.

"Chance I promise you there is no one else in my life. I have always been devoted to you." Stephanie begged him to listen.

"I know you have been visiting the Doc behind my back." Chance screamed at her.

"It's not what you think."

"What am I supposed to think? You belong to me."

Stephanie paced back and forth. There was no denying she was scared. She had seen Chance out of control but this was so much worse than before. She knew there was no winning this fight. To stay, would only mean things would turn physical and Stephanie already bore the scars that were evidence of that. She had to get out of the barn and away from Chance.

Stephanie's brain raced, looking for a way to escape. As she turned, Chance blocked the door. She was trapped and there was no escape. Stephanie turned her back to Chance, as she was walking to the blanket where they had been sitting. It was her last mistake.

Before Stephanie could take more than two steps, she felt the blow from behind, and her world went dim. Darkness fell over her eyes as she hit the floor. She heard footsteps in the hay as she faded from awareness. She never saw Chance pick up the pitch fork.

Before...

"So, tell me all about your hot date last night!" Hillary giggled as she swung around the metal door frame that opened into Stephanie's office.

"What's to tell? I went, it was horrible... I hated every minute of it and I couldn't wait to get home and watch TV with my cat." Stephanie hung her head in shame, slyly looking up over the top of her glasses. This was not the first time she came to work on a Monday morning and had to tell the agony of her horrible dates to Hillary. It had become a horrible tradition and she had become jaded about the whole idea of dating. It was not for lack of her trying, but dating in New York City was not easy for a woman who wanted to find a man and fall in love.

Hillary lowered her head and moved to the rear of Stephanie's desk wrapping her arms around her as she put her head down on his desk and began to bang it up and down. "Oh Hill, is there something wrong with me? I try so hard, and have definitely done my share of comparison shopping, but I always end up with guys who want to sleep with me, or that are jerks…or ones who just need mental evaluations." Stephanie covered her eyes with both hands and waited for the speech from Hillary, that she knew was coming.

And then it came … "Stephanie you are a great girl. We have talked about this a million times. And you would be such a catch for any good man. Believe me, I wish I was a man, I would date you. I should be so lucky. Trust me, if I don't find a good man myself, I am going lesbian. I will find a really big butch dyke and settle down. They still use dildos…right?" Hillary laughed uncontrollably out loud and hugged Stephanie tighter. "You're a hot woman and so worth dating. I think men just think with their dicks too much. Women do the same thing; they just think with ... um ... something else."

Stephanie held on tight to her friend's embrace. "What would I do without a best friend like you to root me on in life?" she smiled at Hillary. "Beats the hell out of me!" She laughed. "But seriously I think you need a break from all this. You are trying too hard, and you are so overworked. It's not good for you sweetheart. Take some time off and find yourself ... before you kill yourself. Go somewhere and get your head together."

Stephanie looked off into space. Her words had sunk in, and she knew Hillary was right. Through her window she gazed at the skyscrapers and skyline. She thought about it, and the fact she had not taken a vacation in over five years. It wasn't the worst idea. "Ok, you sold me on it, but where should I go? I don't want to take time off and just hang out in Manhattan."

Hillary thought about it and walked back and forth a few times. She thought to herself ... 'What was the one place that could make her forget about everyday life?' And then it came to her, "Maybe some place sunny and hot." Stephanie looked up at her, "Why sunny and hot?" "Because in sunny hot places the men take off their clothes, and you can see what you are getting before you totally waste your time. Nothing like seeing a man's junk in a speedo, you know." She laughed. "Besides you have an amazing body. Not that I was peaking, but all those trips to the gym have paid off. Maybe if you just took off the glasses, put in some contacts, and let your hair down." As Hillary laid the glasses on the desk and looked at what she had done, Stephanie had become so different, she was sexy, almost a different person.

Hillary snapped out of her thoughts as Stephanie spoke, "I guess a hot man in a speedo wouldn't be so bad." Stephanie smiled and her mind wondered. She visualized the mostly naked men, walking back and forth on the beach. All of their bodies glistening in the sun, looking for just the right woman to spend their vacation with. She liked the idea for about ten seconds. Stephanie's head raised and as her eyes caught Hillary's; her expression screamed mistake. "I can't do it, those guys at the beach, would be just as bad as the ones here in the city. I need some place where I can rest and reenergize, and find guys who are worth meeting." Hillary sarcastically snapped at her, "Why don't you just go to Arizona and find yourself a cowboy."

Stephanie spun around in her chair. Her eyes brightened and a smile stretched from ear to ear. "That's it! I have always loved the old west and cowboys. Why not book a vacation at a ranch? I could get away from everything."

"Yeah, like all modern conveniences and good cell reception." Hillary snapped at her, "Look Stephanie, I know you … I love you, and you, without the internet and cell service, would not be pretty. Sweetheart, have you ever experienced a panic attack?"

"I can do this. I know I can. I can make it without the net and text messages. It'll be hard, but I am a strong person. I can go off the grid for a minute. A total change … that is all I want."

"You, off the grid for five minutes … No … you will be pulling out all the beautiful blond hair of yours. Besides, you don't stand a chance in hell of finding a man in the desert. Why would you think such a thing? What are you going to do, meet one in a ghost town in the middle of nowhere?" She shook her head.

"Well, if there is ghost town near where I am staying, I will be glad to check it out. I'm going!" She snapped back.

"You're just talking; it will never happen." Hillary smirked at her.

"Don't believe me… I am going online right now. See right here West Fork Ranch. They have rooms to rent on a functioning ranch."

Hillary looked her dead in the face, "You are not going to do this. Please tell me you are not. They have snakes, and desert, and bad things to hurt you there." A look of fear crossed her face, "For god's sake, all the product in the world will not save your hair after the sweating you will do there. You will be wet, messy, covered in sand, and … well my love, I don't know how else to say this … you will stink. No man will want you if you stink. Well, unless he has a weird fetish. Look, I am sorry I pushed you; let's think about this some more."

"Too late Hill, my mind is made up."

"Don't do it. I'm begging you. Think about your hair."

"My information is already in the system I just have to hit enter."

"You can't do it."

"I just did."

"Oh my God, you did! What fresh hell have you unleashed?"

Stephanie smiled up at Hillary over her computer monitor with a sly expression on her face. She looked as if she were a cat, who had just eaten the family's canary. Hillary moved around to the side of the desk, and looked on in disbelieve. "You aren't joking... you really did it. If I was religious, I would pray for your soul right now." Her jaw dropped when she fully understood Stephanie was going. She looked up at her, "Where can we buy you a snake bite kit?"

They both laughed and realized what a step she had taken. Hillary's face lit up with possibilities. "It'll be too hot for chaps. Even with the ass cut out; I think it would not work. Too much sweat, too much roughness on your skin, it would leave marks. I wonder if we can find you a leather thong, that says Rough Rider on it?" Stephanie looked puzzled at first, then smiled as if the idea suited her. She pursed her lips together as she typed the words into the search engine. "You know my ass would look really great in something like that." Stephanie laughed. "You know it, right!" Hillary replied.

Mullins

Chapter One: Arizona Here I Come

Stephanie left work that evening like a woman on a mission. If she was going through with this trip, she wanted new clothes that read ranch hand. Or at least said casual country. She had worked in Manhattan since she had finished grad school. She was now 28 years old, and settled into the life of a business executive. The most casual thing she ever wore were khaki shorts or jeans.

She hit store after store and wore herself ragged, trying to find cowboy wear in the big city. Finally, she faced the realization, it was not going to happen. She walked aimlessly down the crowded street. Then she walked by the last place she ever expected to ever go in, the Goodwill. A desperate feeling entered her body. 'How can

I ever go into a place like this?' She thought to herself. She walked forward three times, and on the fourth she stopped dead in her tracks, staring into the doorway. She tilted her head to the side and thought for a minute. "I can do this; I know I can. Where else could I find worn in jeans and t-shirts?"

Stephanie browsed through the racks, and to her surprise found many big named labels. "Who knew you could find expensive shirts here?" She sarcastically whispered to herself, as she weeded through. In the stack, she found just what she wanted. Button down shirts and jeans that fit her butt so well, she had to glance twice in the mirror at how good it looked. She smiled and thought to herself, "I'd hit this."

Stephanie went to the register with the pile of clothes she picked out. As the girl rang her up, Stephanie looked at the total in disbelieve. The girl told her the amount and Stephanie just looked at her, expecting she had made a mistake. For a woman who would spend hundreds of dollars on an outfit, to take home a week's worth of clothes for less than seventy-five dollars was mind boggling.

As she walked to the subway, she felt the weariness of the day catching up with her. A quick stop by her favorite Chinese place, would ensure she could just crash when she got home. Nothing to do but entertain her cat, and sort through her new clothes.

Stephanie was just in the door as she felt the familiar rubbing of her best friend around her calves. She looked down and saw the fuzzy gray tail of Samantha, her short haired cat, going between her legs. Samantha was just a couple of months old when Stephanie had adopted her for companionship, but now two years later she ruled the house. When she brought Samantha home, the task of naming the little ball of fur was easy; she was watching an episode of Bewitched, and it just all worked out. Now she couldn't imagine life without her.

As she sat down her packages on the counter, Stephanie reached down and pulled Samantha up to her chest. Samantha rubbed her face against Stephanie's mouth wanting to be kissed. "Samantha my dear, how would you handle a few days away from mommy?" She asked. Samantha instantly gave her reaction, as with anything she did not like. She made a stressed meow that sounded like the word "no". Stephanie looked down into her eyes and the guilt ran through her body. "You know I love you, but I think Auntie Hill is going to house sit with you for a little while."

She sat down on the couch and pulled open her laptop. This had been a usual routine for years now. Check the email to see if anyone had contacted her… they usually had not. Read through her usual sites, to see if there were updates. Go on the adult dating sites, and see if anyone looked interesting. And then go on an adult blog, and worship as many naked men as possible. "This must end!" She looked at Samantha as if she understood her. This is crazy, you can't shake the whore tree to find marriage material." That being said, she closed her laptop and tossed it to the side of the couch. "I don't care what

Hill says, I can unplug for a week. I've been without the internet before, and phone too. Remember when the power went out a year ago during the brownout. I survived. No, really, I did, for four straight hours. I was OK…until Hillary made it over here." She said quietly looking a lot like a small child, as she hugged one of the pillows from the couch. "I can be strong. I know I can. Hmm, I wonder if they have sushi in the desert. Because there is no way I am eating red meat."

Mullins

Chapter Two: I'm Heading West

After several days of waiting, the date arrived. It was time for Stephanie to go out into the real world. Hillary arrived early to her apartment ready to cheer her on. As she knocked on the front door, Samantha hid behind a chair, so she could see what was going on. This was the typical routine when Hillary arrived. The cat hated her, no one knew why. Maybe it was the routine that was destined to happen when they came face to face. And then it happened, Hillary saw the grey tail sticking out from behind the chair and went for it.

As she grabbed for the cat, it happened. There was that sound you hear on TV when something happens to a cat, and they sound like they are being stepped on or scared to death. That long shriek of fear, that blasts out loud terrifyingly, and you laugh for some reason, and you don't know why you are doing it. Samantha had perfected the noise and it was reserved for Hillary.

The noise did not slow Hillary for a minute; she just scooped up the cat, and started her usual routine of pretending she was a baby … complete with baby talk. "You know she hates when you do that." Stephanie shook her head. "Nonsense, she loves her Auntie Hillary." And with that, Hillary squeezed and hugged the cat, as it hissed and made a deep throated growling noise. Samantha held out for a few minutes until she just couldn't take it anymore. Then she pulled out her tried and true escape route. She quieted down for a minute and raised a paw. Slowly the claws came out and Hillary saw them. Freedom had been achieved.

"So, are you all packed?" She asked. "Yeah, just need to get a couple of things from the bathroom and put in my lenses." Stephanie replied. Returning to the bathroom, she grabbed what she needed and returned contacts in, dressed down in her new jeans and a t-shirt. As she walked through the door, Hillary stepped back for a second and gasped. "Are you Ok?" She asked. "Yeah sure, it's just such a change. You look like an entirely different person. If I didn't know it was you, I would swear you had a sister. The glasses and clothes make such a difference." "So, this is better?" She asked. "Uh Huh!" Hillary mumbled swallowing hard.

"Ok, so let's go through the check list. You have your clothes, underwear, socks, and boots. What about other essentials? Do you have lube?" Hillary smiled in a way that was so evil Stephanie cringed. "Be serious Hill." "I am serious, you don't date much, and sweaty hot desert sex might be a bit rough. Better sticky than painful you know." Stephanie just looked at her in disbelief. "Ok already, I have condoms and lube. I even have some sexy underwear. I'm just not sure about a thong in the desert." "You'll be fine, just don't get any sand up your butt cheeks." She giggled not believing she had said it out loud.

Hillary walked around Stephanie several times observing the change in her. Each time she shook her head. "Ok Hill, you are giving me a complex. What is wrong with this? Do I look weird or something?" She asked crossing her arms and looking very uncomfortable. "Nothing is wrong; I just never pictured you like this before. I bet if you walked through Central Park looking like this, you would have to beat guys off of you." "That good ... really?" She asked. "No, that great. You look amazing.

Aww ... I feel like one of those parents on the 60's sitcoms, that just discovered their daughter was beautiful, and they just became scared to death about some boy jumping on her. It's just like you are about to go off to your prom." "I never went to my prom you know." Stephanie chimed in. "Why does this not surprise me?" "I just didn't want to support the lie that I had to be the perfect little cheerleader." "Amen sister, but didn't you have a cousin you could have gone with, and just hang out to be with your friends." "Again, that was not who I wanted to be. And you know I was in high school way before it would have been cool to buck the system. Back then it would not have ended very pretty." Her face grew a little dimmer at the thought.

Hillary moved behind her, as she looked into the mirror. "Do you really think I am hot like this?" "Oh god yeah! Now let's talk about S.E.X." Hillary never spoke the word normally. She always acted as if it was a dirty word and mouthed it in a mocking way. "What was that? You want to talk about what?" "S.E.X. You heard me the first time." "No, I heard you mumble a word that you cannot say aloud." Stephanie smiled in her devilish way that could melt anyone's heart. She sat on the bed and patted her hand on the spot beside herself. Hillary sat down, "Look I think we need to talk about S.E.X. I am really serious about this." "Why do you think this?" She asked. "Because I don't think you are doing it right. Let's face it, you've had a lot of squatters in your flat, but no one has moved in permanently.

Stephanie laughed and shook her head. "Hill, I know how to have sex. And the reason I don't have a boyfriend is my own choice. I want a man I can marry one day, not someone who is just in for the weekend. I want a pretty face I can wake up to every morning, not one I just sat down on last night. I will be fine. But not if I miss my plane, the ticket is non-refundable." "Ok, let's get this show on the road. Throw what's left in your bag and kiss the cat, we are out of here."

As Stephanie left the building, she was already feeling guilty about leaving Samantha. She was sure Hillary would do a great job of taking care of her. And she knew Samantha was safe, but the poor cat would have non-stop Hillary for over a week. It was so unfair, she decided on the way home, she would buy a calming collar. Maybe that would help Samantha to forgive for at least a minute.

Stephanie piled her bags in the back of the taxi and turned to Hillary. "Take care of my cat." She smiled at her. "And take care of you as well." Hillary beamed at her as if her whole world lit up. "What will I do without you for so long?" "Hill, it will be just over a week." "Shut up! I am having one of those Hollywood moments. You know where they have some grand good-bye and everyone cries." "You will never be right Hill. You know that, don't you?" "But of course, I'm not only an amazing friend but also a drama queen." The cab driver chimed in with is thick Bronx accent, "Well, Your Highness, if you are about done. It is rush hour, and your friend here has to make it all the way across the city to the airport. So, unless you want her to miss her plane, wrap it up." "What an unpleasant little man." Hillary said as she smirked and imitated the Queen of England. "Remind me to kill him later. But for now, give me a kiss and go before I really do break out the water works."

Stephanie climbed into the cab just getting seated, as the cabbie gunned the engine. "Your friend is some piece of work. Is she always like that?" Stephanie looked up at the cabbie shaking her head and saying only one word, "Unfortunately." And then after a brief moment of silence, "She single, you think I could get her number?"

Stephanie thought about it for a moment and used her better judgement and did not give out her number. She didn't think Hillary was ready to be a cab driver's wife.

The cab arrived at the airport almost an hour later. Traffic had been horrible and Stephanie was ready to get out of the cab. For most of the trip she had invented little games to distract herself from the cabbie's pleading for Hill's phone number. Her last games had started to gross herself out, especially when she had gotten to 'guess that stain' and 'what is that odor'. She was OK until he realized that the stains and odors were all around her and the seat beneath her was covered as well. She was sure of one thing; the used condom on the back floorboard, did not make her feel too comfortable as to what had recently happened in the back seat.

Stephanie thanked the cabbie who once again asked for Hill's phone number. Stephanie just smiled and headed to the outer door. "You talk to your friend and see what she says, if she is interested just call the cab company and have them send Hank over to her place." The cabbie called out as Stephanie waved a hand over her shoulder while trying to contain herself.

The check-in, was not as bad as she had thought it would be and she was boarded in a decent amount of time. Stephanie was cautious the whole time while she was in the airport and getting seated on the plane. She had remembered all the news reports of terrorist activities. In her mind, she kept chanting the same thing over and over, 'please don't let me get killed just because I needed a vacation.' In time she settled in, and tried to get comfortable, but her head kept racing with totally useless information. She tried to put her fears aside and then she thought of Hill, maybe she was right about panic attacks.

She cleared her head, meditated for a minute and thought 'What's the worst thing that could happen? I get stuck next to some big smelly guy who won't shut up and tries to use me as a pillow.' She smiled and then felt a tap on her shoulder. "Hi, I think I am supposed to be by the window." Stephanie looked up to say 'Excuse me.' But the words got trapped in her throat. There before her stood a very huge man who smelled of garlic and onions. Stephanie cleared her throat, stood up to move into the aisle, and let the man squeeze in. As she returned to her seat Stephanie sarcastically laughed and said, "What took you so long?"

As the plane took off, Stephanie wondered if this was all a big mistake. So far everything was not as she imagined. She wanted to talk to Hill so badly. She was the only one who could calm her down. She fumbled into her pocket and freed her cell phone and to her surprise it had a signal. The steward explained that she was welcome to use her phone during the flight just not take-off and landing times. A feeling of normality flooded her body as she clicked Hillary's number and heard the phone start ringing.

The phone rang several times until she almost gave up, and then the sound she had been wanting so badly was there. "You didn't even make it to Arizona and you are already calling me. Tell Mama what is wrong?" She laughed trying to contain herself. "Just nerves, I guess. Everything has not gone as I imagined, and maybe I am a little scared, when I get there it won't get any better." "Oh pish, you are going to be fine. Traveling sucks and you know that, but when you get there everything will be fine. Just relax." "I wish I could. Remember that problem I told you about when I travel?" She asked. "Oh yeah, you mean the one with the big smelly guy who wants to use you as a mattress?" "A pillow Hillary, a pillow … Well it is happening again. Even as we speak about it." "Poor baby, just shift around and make him as uncomfortable as possible, and he will shift in the other direction." Hillary insisted and Stephanie tried her advice and within a minute the guy was curled up in the opposite direction.

"Now that wasn't so hard was it? What else can Mama do for her little girl?" "Ok Hill, you are starting to creep me out." "I'll stop, but seriously is it all that bad?" Hillary opened up the flood gate and Stephanie turned it all loose. She listened and tried to be supportive, but she knew Stephanie just needed to say it all to someone.

While she listened, Hillary glanced around the room continually looking for the cat. She would turn her attention back and forth between Stephanie and the cat. When she was done and she had said 'uh huh' a hundred times, she felt better. Then she looked down at the cat, which was staring at her intently.

"Stephanie does the cat ever do weird things when you are here alone with her?" "No, not that I know of. What is she doing?" She asked. "I don't know, she started by following me everywhere, but trying to hide as if she wasn't. Then she just started coming out of nowhere and I would turn around and she would be staring at me really weird, like up in my face. I went to the bathroom and was about to go when I turned around, she was on the sink staring, and then suddenly…I didn't need to go. Now she is sitting in front of me licking her claws in a way that says 'I will cut you bitch'. Is this at all normal?"

Stephanie laughed, "No, I can't say I have ever had that happen before. If I were you, I would call the police and tell them your pussy is trying to kill you." "Smart ass, and to think I just sat here and listened to all your problems. I hate you … you know that right? Now get off my cell! And call me when you land so I know you got there safe," "Will do. Oh by-the-way the cab driver asked for your number. Well, begged actually." "Did you give it to him?" Hillary asked. "No, I didn't think you would want me too." "Damn, he was kind of cute, and dirty. I could have done things I would not be proud of." "Don't worry, he said you could call for a cab and ask for Hank." "Get off the phone I need to make a call." Hillary laughed. Stephanie sat back into her uncomfortable seat and the weight of everything seemed to leave her.

Mullins

Chapter Three: A Leather Thong Does Make You Sweat in the Desert

As the plane was about to land Stephanie felt excitement and anticipation. She had finally let go of her anxiety. Deep down inside she knew she could do this. She peered out the window looking over her new friend who had passed out for most of the trip. The landscape was the same for as far as she could see; there was a lot of flat land and no tall buildings. This puzzled her, being a New Yorker; there were tall buildings everywhere you went in the city. The area looked like a dry dusty place, and except for the airport; there was not much to see.

An announcement started as the wheels touched down, "Attention passengers as you depart the plane please remember that although the inside of the plane and the airport are climate controlled, the outside landscape will be a bit of an adjustment. Please be prepared for intense heat. Thank-you for flying with us today." Stephanie cocked her head and wondered how bad it could be. She had been in extreme heat before, and it never bothered her. She was sure she would be alright. The passengers left the plane and headed for the baggage claim. Stephanie was happy to see her bags made it safely and none were missing. Things were looking up.

She studied the signs, trying to find her way to the main entrance. Someone from the ranch was to meet her just out front and drive her in. Stephanie smiled; it was all starting to take shape. Nothing could go wrong at this point she told herself. As she got closer to the front doors, she could feel the heat blowing in like waves as the doors would open and close. "Ok Stephanie, this is just like going to the sauna at home." She whispered to herself. As she approached the door, her friend from the flight and several others gathered around. They all rushed out into the great Arizona sun like children trying to be first in line. One by one, they fell to the ground, as heat and humidity threw them a one-two punch.

Stephanie looked around her as security and staff rushed to their aide. She took a deep breath and realized luck must be on her side since she had not fallen to the pavement with her fellow passengers. She glanced around the parking lot intently trying to locate his ride. Just as she was about to completely give up, she saw the sign on the side of one of the vehicles in the tow-away zone. It had to be for him. She made her way over to it trying to keep up with her bags and not succumb to heat stroke while getting there.

The sun was blinding and beating down on her head. She could feel beads of perspiration starting. "You need a hat my friend." Stephanie heard the voice, but was not sure where it had come from. "Excuse me," She replied turning around in a circle until she found the source of the words. As Stephanie focused, the figure of a man came into view. The more she squinted the clearer the man became. He had been sitting in the back of the vehicle. As the man rounded the corner and reached out to shake Stephanie's hand, she realized the man was stripped down to the waist. His muscular chest glistened with sweat, it was obvious he had been there for a while waiting.

The man smiled and ran his hand over his chest to free the moisture that was dripping down. "I am betting you are the guest I am supposed to be picking up. My name is Joe, and you must be Stephanie." She smiled and looked the man straight in the eyes, "Yes, I am. It's good to meet you." Stephanie felt her heart beating harder with each second. It had been such a long time since any man made her feel this out of control. She felt her mouth start to salivate, but he fought it back. She just stood there grinning not knowing what to say or how to act.

"Man, you sure picked a hell of a day to show up; this is the hottest this summer so far. Just look at you, only here a few minutes and you are soaked through." Joe pulled out a towel from the back of the van as he loaded the bags in. He handed it to Stephanie and looked at her as a huge smile stretched across his face. As she took the towel, their hands brushed each other and Stephanie jerked as if electricity had surged through her body. "Dry off a bit, and I will see if I have an extra hat you can put on. You're from New York City, right?" Joe asked her. "Yeah, I am." "So, what the hell made you think about coming out here? This is about as far from city life as you can get." "I know, that is why I chose here. I needed to get away. I needed a change." Joe pulled out a hat and smacked it over the leg of his jeans and knocked a load of dust out of it. "Well, welcome to the change. I hope this is what you really wanted."

As Joe turned to the back of the vehicle, Stephanie became aware of how well Joe's jeans fit his backside. And then, the salivating started again. 'Men in New York never looked like this.' She thought to herself, cracking a wry smile. "I think this is everything I wanted." Stephanie said, as Joe closed the back door.

As the van pulled out of the airport, it was like leaving the last piece of civilization and heading into the desert. "You don't mind fast driving, do you?" Joe asked as he pushed his foot down further towards the floor. "It's just that we have to go a long way to the ranch, and nobody drives slow out here." Stephanie just smiled at him, captivated by his ripped muscles. It was obvious Joe had worked on, or around ranches his whole life. His body was rugged and toned, and it didn't come from a gym. He worked hard for it...and it showed. Stephanie studied every inch of him, mystified by his perfection. His brown wavy hair suited the tanned look of his skin. Stephanie whispered to herself, "It's definitely getting better." "What's getting better?" Joe asked. "Everything!"

As they drove to the ranch, they passed by large properties along the way covered in cows and oil wells. The landscape was so different from what Stephanie was used to. She felt like she was on a different planet. This was more than she bargained for, but at the same time it was everything she wanted. A chance to break the mundane every day existence of the city; going from apartment to subway, and subway to work and the same old routine day after day. There was nothing familiar about this. She decided she liked it. And she liked her new company. She hoped most of the men who she ran into on this trip, had the same ideas about lack of clothing. Stephanie smiled and wondered what Hill would think of her riding around the desert with a half-naked ranch hand. And then it dawned on her, she was supposed to call when she landed.

"Damn, I forgot to call my friend when I got here, to let her know I made it alright." "Well good luck with that one, you probably won't be able to get a signal until we are near the ranch. Check and see if you want to, but it probably won't work." Stephanie fished out her phone and held it up to look at the screen. It was as she feared, the phone just said searching for signal. She was cut off, just like Hill had said she would be. Funny thing was, she was not panicking and did not feel desperate like when she had it happen in the city. The worst had happened and yet she was excited, maybe it was the new surrounding or maybe it was Joe, but she decided she could handle both, and looked forward to what was to come.

They pulled into the long driveway of the ranch after over an hour of driving. Stephanie was overwhelmed by the size of the place. It was so much more than she expected, and at the same time she was torn about getting out of the small space of the van and leaving Joe. As the van pulled up to the front door; Stephanie looked upon the largest house she had ever seen. The front door opened and out stepped Mona, the owner of the ranch. She was a loud and outgoing woman, who bellowed out Stephanie's name the minute she saw her. "It is so good to have you here Stephanie; I was getting worried about you two." "Thank-you," Stephanie said moving away from the vehicle. "I'm glad to be here. The ranch is beautiful." "Well come on in out of this heat, and I'll get you something to drink and get you settled in."

As Mona led Stephanie inside, Joe followed a little behind with her bags. "This is so different from what I expected." Stephanie smiled at her. "Well what did you expect?" Mona laughed. "I don't know. I have never been any place like this before. But I like it a lot." "Well sweetheart, I am glad you do, and for the time you are here, welcome home and to our family." "Thanks."

Stephanie wondered around the reception area. It was filled with Old West memorabilia. There were guns of all sorts and sizes hanging on every wall, paintings that were authentic to the time period of the Old West, and around the fireplace were several pictures taken of western scenes and cowboys. Being the truly inquisitive person that she was, Stephanie headed straight for the cowboys. Some of the photos depicted life around the ranch in the old days. Much of the scenery was of half stripped cowboys breaking horses or doing work in the yard. And then there were a couple of them that were posed, of men and women together. One man had his arm around a woman.

Stephanie stared at the picture hard like there was something familiar about it. She felt weak inside, and a little queasy for a moment. She looked at the two people, one at a time and studied them. One of the men was ruggedly handsome and had wavy dark hair. His tight muscled body showed through his clothing. He was what anyone would have thought a typical cowboy would look like. Stephanie smiled as she looked at the man. There was a familiar attraction, a feeling like she once knew the cowboy. She felt a pride in how sexy the man was. Confusion welled up inside her, how could Stephanie have ever known anything about a man in a photo she had never seen before?

She then turned to the woman standing on the right side. She looked a bit out of place, not at all comfortable in her western clothing. This woman didn't look at all like she belonged in the old west. Stephanie stared hard at the slightly grainy photo. The woman's hair was very well kept and appeared to be dirty blond and her clothing looked a bit more like modern clothes of another period. As she squinted and focused harder, she stared straight into the woman's pale colored face. And then she saw it, "She looks like me." Stephanie whispered under her breath.

Stephanie ran it through her brain a couple of times trying to figure out how this woman looked so much like her. "Mona ... these photos ... where did they come from?" She asked. Mona looked up from her desk to see what Stephanie was talking about, "What's that my dear? Oh, the photos, they were loaned to us by the Ballin sisters, Miss Mary and Miss Elizabeth. They are a couple of eccentric old ladies, who live next property over from here. Apparently, they were in their family's collection from back in the day. They let us use them to give the place a little bit of history."

Stephanie glared at the photo and then turned to Mona. "This one woman...kinda looks like me." Mona headed over to the fireplace smiling in disbelief. She leaned in and studied the woman's face and then turned back to Stephanie. "Oh my god, you two could have been twins, was this one of your relatives or something?" She asked. Stephanie shook her head no. "Looks like these two were very close. See how the man is holding on to the woman. Maybe they were more than friends." Mona smiled at her in a comforting way. "There were women in the old west you know." Stephanie looked at her with a weird face. "Now, I don't know who she was, but I'm sure the Ballin sisters could tell you. Stop over and see them. They have a story for everything. They are funny old ladies though; one will start a sentence and the other will usually finish it." Mona laughed at the thought and went back to checking Stephanie in.

Chapter Four: Back in the Saddle … Again!

Stephanie settled in at the ranch and the next morning she realized what she had done. How could she have come out to the middle of nowhere? She didn't know how to be in the desert, or anything about being on a ranch. How was she supposed to see the area? They didn't have Metro Cards there. There was no bus or subway. And then she realized the most awful truth of all, there were no coffee shops. She was ready to cry again.

She was at a loss being out of the city and in unfamiliar surroundings. Most of all, she was missing Hillary. She was always around, always there to make her feel at ease. Since she had arrived at the ranch, her phone was quiet. She had checked on the way in, and no reception. She shook her head in disbelief that anyone could live like this. "If this is living off the grid, I want to go home. Back to the sky scrapers, internet and cell towers that work. Just as she was finishing her muttering rant, there was a knock. She opened the door to find Mona smiling in her usual motherly way.

"How are you today, have you settled in sweetheart?" She asked.

"I'm Ok, just feeling cut off from the world, I guess. No phone or internet can be a bit of a shock for a New York City girl"

"We have internet and phone. Just log into the ranch's net and you can use your cell to piggyback and make phone calls. It only works if you are near the property."

"Thank-You Mona!" She said excitedly.

"We are in the desert, but we aren't savages you know. When you get done calling, head on out to the stables, Joe will give you a lesson in riding a horse."

Mona walked away laughing and mumbling under her breath. "Like I could live without the internet."

Stephanie fumbled with her cell to search for a signal. As she ran her finger across the screen, there it was. The ranch showed as an accessible signal. Joy over-ran her; it was as if she had struck oil. She was connected to the outside world once more. Relief filled her as she hit Hill's number, as she had done every day for so many years. The phone beeped once, then twice. 'Maybe it isn't actually working,' she thought. In New York, Hillary sat watching the phone as it blasted ABBA music, "I'll teach you not to phone me when you travel half way across the United States."

Just as the phone was about to go to voice mail, she grabbed it. "You better have a good explanation for why you waited a day to let me know you arrived safely." "Well, actually it was about 13 hours. But I am calling now and I just found out how to get a signal." Stephanie replied. There was a momentary silence on the phone and then Hillary spoke, "Alright, you are forgiven. I have missed you so much. Tell me everything that has happened. Have you ridden a horse or killed any cows for dinner yet?" Stephanie laughed; it was good to have a little bit of familiar life back again.

"No, I haven't killed or ridden anything yet. Mind you there is one ranch hand I might not mind going for a ride on…excuse me…with." She laughed.

"Oh, do tell. Is he that hot?"

"Very much, when I met him at the airport, he was half naked."

"Which half?" Hillary was hooked.

"Well, seriously, he had his shirt off. And I liked it. And I like this place, I guess." Stephanie added.

"You guess? It's what I predicted isn't it? You are cut off from everything 'city' and you don't know what to do with yourself."

"You are right," She sighed. "I am just going to have to go outside my comfort zone. Maybe, I will go horse-back riding."

"Hah, you on a horse, take pictures…I will have to see this." Hillary laughed. "Just be careful and know I miss you like crazy."

"I miss you too and Samantha. How is she doing?"

"About that …." Hillary paused

"Oh god you didn't kill my cat, did you?" Stephanie panicked.

"No, no, she is fine. She is just a little odd. Yes, maybe odd is the right word for this."

"What do you mean odd?" He asked.

"Well, hmm, is she ever aggressive with you?"

"No, why do you ask?"

As Hillary explained the odd behavior; Samantha edged her way across the room. With each word the cat got closer and closer. "It's just that she keeps watching me, and I swear she is plotting my death." As the last words left Hillary's lips she looked down at her feet, where the cat sat staring at her intensely. With a calm calculated move, Samantha lifted her front right paw, and extended all of her claws at once. She stared up at Hillary as she licked each claw. Hillary moved back two steps and stared into the cat's eyes. "Ok Stephanie, now I am sure of it; the cat means me harm. She is licking her claws and thinking how nice it would be to kill me."

"Oh Hill, you are overreacting, she is just getting used to me being gone, and you there alone with her. Just be calm and she will come around." Stephanie reassured her.

"Be calm! The cat wants to cut me like a bitch! Oh god, she is moving towards me; I better get off the phone. I can defend myself better with two hands. Much love, and call me tonight. Oh god, she is running at me." And the phone went dead.

Stephanie started to say goodbye but realized the call had already ended. She thought about it for a second, 'The cat is not dangerous. At least I don't think so.' She smiled shutting the door to her room and headed down the steps to the reception area. As she walked out onto the front porch, the bright hot sun hit her in the eyes. The temperature was pushing one hundred degrees. As her foot touched the first step, Mona ran behind her. "Here honey, sun glasses and some water. You'll need them." Stephanie thanked her and headed over to the stables.

She looked around as she walked, there were more ranch hands than Stephanie had imagined. They all stood before her like cookie cutter versions of cowboys. As she approached the open door of the stable, she heard movement and talking from within, Joe was there brushing a horse and talking to it. He was so loving. Stephanie smiled at him. She was amazed at the idea of this six-foot-tall man with ripped muscles being so gentle. She walked in the door and cleared her throat so Joe would know she was there.

"Hey Joe."

"Hi Stephanie! Did you sleep well?" He asked.

"Yeah, Mona suggested I come out and see you about riding lessons."

"Is that the only reason you came to see me?" Joe asked.

Stephanie laughed, "Well yes, and no."

"So, what was the other reason then?" Joe asked.

"I guess, I just wanted to see you...maybe." Stephanie replied as her face turned red.

"If you don't get over being so shy, we are never going to get to know each other."

"Ok, I wanted to see you, and I am trying to push past my boundaries and learn to ride a horse. I need to get outside my comfort zone." Stephanie said cocking her head sideways trying to look Joe in the eyes.

"Good start. I will teach you to ride this morning. And tonight, we go on a date."

"I think I could handle that."

"Great, now let's talk about these clothes."

"What's wrong with my clothes?" Stephanie asked.

"You look like one of those old western movie cowgirls. Let's lose a few things. Let's start with getting rid of the button-down shirt… don't want you to overheat." By the time Joe was done, Stephanie looked like your typical ranch hand in jeans and t-shirt. "Besides, you are way hotter this way." Joe winked at her.

Stephanie took to horse riding more quickly than she ever imagined. Joe only had to help her get into the saddle. She took the reins and rode the horse into the yard as Joe watched intently. "You sure you never did this before?" "Yeah, I can't explain it. Just seems like something second nature to me." Stephanie rode around the yard several times in the corral, and then outside. Joe shook his head in disbelief. He had never seen anyone take so quickly to riding. "I think you are safe to ride now."

Joe saddled up a second horse for himself and rode up beside Stephanie. "Let's ride out and take a short trip around the property. You want to be in the front or in the back? Personally, I am pretty comfortable either way." Joe grinned at her in a devilish way. Stephanie blushed at the sexual overtone, "I think I want you beside me." Joe rode up beside, and reached out his hand. Stephanie reached out and took it. "You ready for this?" Joe asked. "Yeah I guess." She said nervously. "What's wrong?" Joe asked. "Ah nothing, just I think I need to spend more time in the gym." "Aww, this is just from ranch work, it builds muscles."

Stephanie took the lead and rode her horse out into the open land ahead of them. Her fear had faded completely. As she bounced up and down in the saddle, her mind drifted. What should have been new sensation and a new environment was not. A sense of déjà vu filled her. She knew she had never been in Arizona before, but there was such a feeling within her that she had been. Even the feeling of the saddle felt familiar as she rode harder and faster. Inside she felt as if she had been cut loose, and even an experienced rider like Joe was having trouble keeping up.

As Stephanie rode, it felt as if she was leading the horse to some place familiar. She had acquired a direction. She was drawn towards a canyon in the distance. As she came to the opening, she slowed down. Joe finally caught up with her. "What's up ahead?" Stephanie asked. "Just an old abandoned ghost town. Nothing much to see, but we can go in if you want." "Yeah I do."

As they rode in, Stephanie looked at all the buildings. All of which were in a state of decay. In her mind, she reconstructed them as they would have looked back in their day. In her vision, they came back to life with color and people that once lived there. One by one, the ghosts came back to life and started moving through their everyday existence. Stephanie shook her head in disbelief. Her imagination just wasn't that good. Yet, she knew every color, every sight, and every sound. It scared her for a moment, and then as they rode up to the old stable, her fears were gone.

Stephanie jumped down from the horse and walked over to the falling down building. Joe came up behind. "Are you OK? He asked. "Yeah, this just all seems like a place I have been before. Thing is, I have never been anywhere like this…that I can remember." She got quiet for a second. Then she walked past the wooded heap, to the building next door. As she got closer, she felt her skin crawl. There was someone watching them. She scanned the windows, but saw no one. Then she looked into the lower level, and saw what could only be described as a dark shadow.

The figure stared out at her. It didn't hide or fade from view. And as Stephanie got closer, she could feel the energy coming from it. It was one of desire, a familiar attraction. She felt drawn to it somehow. Joe came up behind her and looked at the building.

"Did you see something?" He asked.

"Yeah...I did, but I think it is gone now. It was there until you walked up."

"What was it?"

"I don't know. I thought it was a person, but it just disappeared into the shadows of the house. It's gone now, but I still feel like I know this place. Even the figure was familiar. I don't know how to explain it." Stephanie looked at Joe in confusion.

"I think you have been out in the heat too long; let's head back." Joe tried to comfort her by putting his arm around Stephanie's shoulders. As they turned away, the figure reappeared in the window. This time it was not just looking on in a curious fashion, it was becoming angry. Seeing Stephanie being touched by Joe enraged it.

Joe led Stephanie away, and helped her onto the horse, and the two were on their way home. Neither of them looked back, nor saw the dark shadowy form that leered at them. They did not see the darkness take form and walk out of the doorway. In the dust behind them stood the figure of a man with dark wavy hair, who was dressed in western clothing.

As the figure walked out off of the porch, the whole town started to change. A swirl of wind blew through the town resurrecting what once was. The ghosts of the dead rose, and took human form again. The buildings rebuilt themselves, and came alive in bright colors. The ghost town became alive again, as if the shadows of the dead found a source of energy and fed off of it.

Chapter Five: Tea and a History Lesson with the Ballin Sisters

Stephanie was more confused than ever when she arrived back at the ranch. She didn't know what she had seen in the ghost town. The name alone invoked a question, she was not even sure of the answer to. Did she believe in ghosts? She had always been open to new things and different ideas, but this was one thing she could not wrap her mind around.

As they dismounted, Stephanie threw her leg around the horse, as if she had been doing it her whole life. Joe just stood in front of her and looked puzzled. "How did you know to do that?" Joe asked. "Do what?" Stephanie looked at him not knowing what he meant. "You threw yourself off that horse like someone who had been riding their whole life." Stephanie looked at the horse and back at Joe, she had no answer. "I guess I just saw someone do it on TV before. I don't really know."

Stephanie turned away, looking out into the desert. Her mind was still in the ghost town, and the figure that she could not explain. She started to walk away not really knowing where she was going.

"Are you OK? You have been acting pretty weird since the town." Joe asked.

"I think I am alright, just a little confused is all. I guess too much at once." Stephanie lied. Being from New York City, there was never too much going on.

"Are we still on for tonight?"

"What?" Stephanie whispered out of her confusion.

"I think we had a date. At least, I hope we did." Joe looked bashful as he spoke.

"Sure, I would like that. What did you have in mind?"

"That's a surprise. You'll have to wait and see."

"OK, I think I can handle that. By the way, do you know the Ballin sisters?"

"Yes, next ranch over. Why?" Joe asked.

"Mona said I should visit them, to ask about some of the pictures in the house."

"Just go out the main gate and turn right, and into the next driveway. It is a bit of a walk, and since you are already hot, I can get you an ATV to use."

"Thanks, that would be great. Say in 20 minutes?" Stephanie asked.

"Sure, no problem."

Stephanie headed into the main house to clean up. She felt as if she was coated in dust and sweat. There was no way she was going to meet a couple of old ladies looking like she did. She headed up to her room, pulled out new clothes, and jumped in the shower. The feel of the cool water did her good. As it rippled over her shoulders and down her chest, she felt the tensing of her aching muscles. She had put herself through more exercise, than a trip to the gym. It was a good feeling though. She had cut loose and pushed herself farther than her normal routine.

As she glanced down at the bottom of the tub, pools of grit and dust joined with the water. With each splash of the shower head, she felt lighter and more relaxed. For a moment, she wasn't worried about being out of her comfort zone, or being with strangers. She felt calm and happy. She had found a place where she didn't have to live up to other people's expectations.

Stephanie walked out of the shower dripping wet and stood in front of the full-length mirror. As she looked at her skin, she could see the redness and color that had formed from her wild ride. The color looked good on her. In the city she was usually pale, and wasn't in the sun that much. This was a nice change. As she looked into the mirror, she studied her face and thought about the woman in the photo down stairs. Their faces were so similar. The other woman had her hair up, but her eyes were exactly the same. "How could two people be so similar?" Stephanie asked out loud.

Stephanie dressed and headed down the stairs. She was a little scared to just walk up two a stranger's door and ask questions, but if she wanted answers, she had no other choice. As she headed out the main door, the ATV waited just beside the steps. Stephanie wasn't much for driving since she lived in the city, and never drove anywhere. It was just another added part of this adventure. This trip really had become an adventure. She was so much outside of her comfort zone, but was beginning to like it.

Stephanie started up the ATV and hit the gas. A cloud of dust and rock flew behind as she peeled out and spun its tires. "This is a learning experience." She said to herself. Her grip tightened as the vehicle flew down the long driveway. She realized that a new obsession with speed was forming within. The horse, was just a jumping off point. As she flew down the drive, a mile-long trail of dust moved through the area coating all who stood near her wake.

She slowed down just long enough to slide around the corner and hit the main road, then she was flying again. In just about two miles, she saw the large sign hanging on the wooden fence saying "Ballin Ranch." She slowed down to a respectable speed, before heading in their entry way. In her mind she rehearsed how she would say hello to the older women. Stephanie didn't want to offend them in any way. She just wanted answers. Something about this, seemed so out of place.

As she slowed the vehicle at the edge of the front porch, she could hear an older woman humming and singing somewhere in the distance. It started off low and then it grew louder. Stephanie couldn't understand a word of what was being sung. The song itself seemed made up and unintelligible. As she listened for the bursts of words and hum, she managed to lock in on a direction. The sounds were coming from behind the house.

She rounded the corner and to her surprise a little old lady popped up from a bush that she had been pruning. She stared at Stephanie intently, and cocked her head to one side. "Who're you?" She said mid hum. "No wait, I know you. I know that face. Give me a minute, I will come up with it. She turned toward the house and went to the back door. "Sister, we have a visitor." Inside the house a loud booming voice responded. It sounded angry and unwelcoming. Stephanie slouched down a bit, fearful of what was coming out to greet her.

"What is this nonsense Sister? You know we do not have visitors!" Miss Elizabeth exclaimed.

"But Sister, we do have a visitor." Miss Mary responded.

"Visitor ... where....Sister?"

"Visitor ... there...Sister!" Miss Mary pointed at Stephanie.

"Hello ... I am S..." Stephanie blurted out before being cut off.

"I know who you are. You are Stephanie." Miss Elizabeth spoke talking over her. "Well, where have you been? You are late."

"Late for what? I don't understand. I just arrived yesterday." Stephanie tried to explain.

"She looks like 'her' Sister." Miss Mary spoke in a soft accented voice.

"He does indeed Sister." Miss Elizabeth studied her face. "We will need tea to get through this."

Miss Mary took Stephanie's hand and led her into the back door. She was almost scared to go inside. She did not know if they were sane or just eccentric. Miss Mary led her to the front parlor and waved an arm as if she were to sit down. Stephanie looked around the room at all the old antiques, it was a collection of a lifetime. The room was filled with things from every decade the old ladies had lived through, and a few from their father's time.

Miss Mary explained to her that the sisters had lived in the house their whole life, like their father before them.

The house had been handed down from one generation to the next for over 250 years. Their father "the Judge" was a well-respected member of society back in the day. Miss Mary smiled as she pointed to the large painting of him on the wall above the fireplace. "I miss Papa ever so much. Since Elizabeth and I never married and Papa died, we are all that is left of the original family."

Stephanie smiled and politely listened as the younger Miss Ballin ran through the whole history of their family, the area and the locals. She even pulled out a photo album with pictures in it that went back over one hundred years. She flipped through the pages one by one going back further and further in time. It was then she hit the old west photos. Stephanie stared intently and scanned each face she saw. Then she found what she was looking for, just as the older Miss Ballin burst through the door with her cart of tea and cakes.

"Sister, why did you pull out all this old stuff? You are only making a mess."

"But Sister, she wants to know." Miss Mary replied.

"Know what Sister?" Miss Elizabeth asked.

"Why, about the old photos of course. Isn't that why you are here my dear?"

"Yes, but how did you know that? Did Mona call you?" Stephanie asked.

"Why no dear, we knew it was time for you to show up. The anniversary is coming you know." Miss Mary replied.

"Anniversary of what Miss Ballin?" She asked

"Here, have some tea and cake dear." Miss Mary insisted.

"Miss Ballin, what anniversary?"

"Oh, please call me Mary." She replied.

"What anniversary?" She insisted.

"Why... the one where you died dear." Miss Mary blurted out.

"I am not dead, I'm quite alive." Stephanie insisted.

"Y'are now...but you weren't then." Miss Elizabeth blasted into the conversation.

"Ok, you are giving me a headache...one of you, either of you; explain to me what you are talking about." Stephanie pleaded.

Miss Mary pulled the photo album over to Stephanie's lap and pointed to the page where she had seen the photo of the woman who looked like her. "See this was you back then with Chance. You were with him when you died." Miss Mary took her hand and told her the story of the relationship she and Chance had shared, and how one hundred years ago she had died in a fire.

She turned the page to reveal even more pictures of this woman from the past. "Her name was Stephanie." Miss Elizabeth interjected. "Our family knew her well. Or should I say, knows you well ... I guess." Stephanie stared at the woman. How could all this be true? She never lived in the old west, and she did not believe in reincarnation.

Stephanie sat back and sipped her tea. In her mind, she had already decided these eccentric old ladies were nuts. They had been alone for far too long, with no one to talk to. She was ready to make a break for it when Miss Mary put her hand on Stephanie's and smiled. "You know he is still out there looking for you." "Who is still out there?" Stephanie asked. "Why Chance of course." Miss Elizabeth blurted out. "He has been looking for you all these years. And now that the anniversary is approaching and you have come here, we have seen him."

Stephanie stood up and walked towards the door. Her mind was racing with all she had heard. How could this be true? It had to be a coincidence or something. She shook her head from side to side, and looked back at the sisters. "I don't understand any of this. It's all too much to take in." "You don't have to take it in, it is fact." Miss Elizabeth snapped at her. "Sister … Be civil, she doesn't understand yet what is happening." Miss Mary stood up to her elder sister. She walked over and held tight to Stephanie's hand.

"It's OK my dear. It's a lot to take in. We have had longer to understand his coming. He has been looking for you for so long, and now since the anniversary is coming, we have even seen him. Out in the garden, he walks around looking all over. Sounds like he is talking to himself. I think since he never passed over, he is still trying to put things in order. He feels bad that you died. Now, since it is the anniversary, he has come back to put it all to rest."

Stephanie looked her in the eyes and asked. "Put it to rest how?"

"Well your death dear. He wants to reunite with you." Miss Mary explained.

"But, I am not dead!" Stephanie exclaimed.

"Nobody's perfect." Miss Elizabeth blurted out.

"Look, I don't remember dying, or this other life or even Chance. This can't be true."

"It's like a prophecy. No matter how hard you fight against it, it's bound to happen." Miss Mary stroked her hand gently.

"I don't want to die. I can't die. I'll fight this." Stephanie insisted.

"Yes, you will, and I pray you will win." Miss Mary turned away from her.

"What did this man look like that you saw in the garden?" Stephanie asked.

"He starts out like a dark shadow and as he moves around, he takes the features he had when he was alive. Just look at the pictures." Miss Elizabeth explained.

Stephanie walked around the room. She had to get out, and go back to the ranch. This was all too much to process. She thanked the sisters for their hospitality and excused herself. As she left, they told her to come back as soon as she could deal with it, and they would help her in any way they could. Stephanie walked down the front steps, and as she reached for the ATV, she felt Miss Mary put a hand on her back. She turned around, and Miss Mary wrapped her arms around her. As confused as she was, this gesture of kindness meant so much to her and touched her heart.

She started up the ATV and raced back to what had become familiar ground to her. As she left the end of the sister's driveway, a cloud of dark swirling wind formed in the back garden. The shape started out as a funnel, but soon took a more solid human form. Out from the wind stepped a man. He was dark at first, and then his face and other parts of his body came to life. He was a dark wavy-haired man. He was tall and handsome. He raised his head up just as Stephanie drove out of view. His dark eyes squinted looking out into the desert. He opened his mouth, but unlike before, he did not moan. From his lips came something clear and unmistakable. He said one word... "Soon."

Mullins

Chapter Six: Time After Time

Stephanie raced for the stables, nearly tipping the ATV, as she rounded the fence. As her mind went in all directions; she played over and over again what the sisters had told her. She thought of herself as open minded, but this was too much to believe. How could she be the reincarnation of this woman from over a hundred years ago? Her mind was in overload, as she plowed into the stable area almost hitting Joe.

"Slow down speed demon. It wasn't rented by the hour?" Joe yelled out.

Stephanie looked at him in shock, "I am so sorry. I didn't realize I was going that fast or getting that close to you."

"Are you alright? You look shaken. Those old ladies didn't convince you to drink any of that family made wine, did they? Their stuff is brutal."

"No, nothing like that. They just scared me."

"Scared you how?" Joe asked.

"They said I was the reincarnation of a woman who lived here before, and it was coming up on the anniversary of my death. And someone who I was in love with back then, was rising up from the dead to come for me."

"Oh … you know the story huh?"

"What do you mean, I know the story? You know this too, how many other people around here have heard about this and didn't bother to tell me?" Stephanie screamed angrily.

"Look Stephanie, we have all heard the stories from the old sisters but we never take them seriously. They are just a couple of sweet eccentric old ladies who believe in ghosts and legends."

"I'm sorry, but eccentric does not fully describe the way those two scared the hell out of me. They wanted me to think I was going to die. And that woman who looked like me; how is that possible?" Stephanie's mind raced to the images of her counterpart.

"First of all…you look like her, since she was here first. Secondly, we all have someone somewhere that kinda looks like us. But if you want to scare the hell out of yourself, just think of her as your doppelganger. Personally, I think you should just calm down and let it all go. Stories of the past and pictures of a woman that looks like you, cannot and will not kill you."

"Oh, and did I tell you that they said the ghost of my lover in the past, has been visiting their garden waiting to reclaim me for himself." Stephanie pulled back, and widened her eyes looking pissed.

"Ok…that I did not know. That is just crazy and we should not even be taking this seriously. I think you need some rest. Go to your room and let this all go. I'll talk to

Mona, and get you some food made up. Maybe we could put our date off to another night when things are less crazy?"

Stephanie agreed and headed back inside the main house. Her head was pounding more with every step. She was having so much trouble putting this behind her. As Joe raced up, Stephanie stopped Mona from asking a hundred different questions that she could not handle. Stephanie walked past, as Joe explained to her what was going on. Mona's mouth dropped wide open as she tried to mutter words, "No, she can't be the one. Are you sure?" Stephanie heard every word, and every bit of the fear in Mona's voice, resonated in her brain.

Stephanie stripped off most of her clothes, hit the bed, and tried to block it all out. She picked up her cell phone. It was time for Hillary. She could always make Stephanie feel better. As she ran her finger over the screen, she saw the flashing. Hillary had beaten her to the phone. As the message started to play, Hillary's unusual voice made her smile. "I think the cat has gone insane. She refuses to eat whatever food I put down. I am under the impression she thinks I am trying to poison her. This is ironic since the war we had yesterday, which I won by the way, she has conceded defeat. But really, I would never poison a prisoner. I would just beat her daily. Oh great, now she has run off to hide again. Does this cat speak English? I obviously do not speak cat, since all I can get out of her is the word "no". Call when you get this, you know I love you. Kisses!"

Stephanie laid her head back and was about to relax, as the knocking started at the door. She cracked it slightly since she had very little on, and saw Joe's beautiful hazel eyes beaming at her. "I have some food for you. Can I come in?" Stephanie backed up a bit and let him enter. As Joe sat down the tray of food on the side of the bed, he turned to see Stephanie standing stripped down to her underwear.

Joe studied her, as a smile crossed his face. Stephanie looked so much better than Joe could have imagined. She had a very nice build for someone who just frequented a city gym. She had the body of a runner. This totally contradicted what Joe had expected. In his mind, Stephanie was a bit of a nerd, who was pale and needed to get out more. Joe was impressed, all the way from her chest to the curve of her legs.

"You know, my eyes are up here." Stephanie laughed. "I always thought that was the best woman's line. …Never thought I would use it."

"I am so sorry, it's just that you are so beautiful. I never thought you would look like this."

"Keep it up, and you might never see any of this again." Stephanie laughed.

"Oh my god, I was so rude. Please excuse anything I said wrong. I am an idiot. … An idiot who does not date much. And now you know why."

"You are forgiven. Up until recently, I was pretty scrawny and pale. Thanks to a gym membership, I am looking a lot better." Stephanie turned to look in the mirror. "Maybe the ghost won't like me if I keep tanning or get muscular."

"I don't know what he likes, but I like you just how you are." Joe responded.

"Really? I had the worst time meeting guys in the city. Too many jerks just looking for sex or whatever. I just gave up on dating. But since I have come here, I have met a guy who I think is everything a girl could want. Oh, and I have a ghost who can't wait to get his hands on me. I think my luck is changing"

"Let the ghost go. I won't give you up without a fight."

"I think you like me." Stephanie giggled trying to hide her embarrassment.

"Yes, I do, now calm down, eat your food and get some rest."

Joe headed for the door, as Stephanie walked near him. They both reached for the door handle at the same time and their hands brushed each other. There was a spark, that sent a chill through both of them. As their eyes met, there were no words to describe the feeling, one that was mutual. Stephanie looked down as Joe raised his hand upwards. His fingers brushed Stephanie's cheek and a rush of red-hot sensation filled her face. Joe gently held Stephanie's chin in his hand, as he raised it and they kissed. Their bodies became one as they held each other.

"Eat your food and rest and we will talk later." Joe whispered as he left the room.

"You sure you don't want to stay? Stephanie asked.

"If I did, you wouldn't be eating or resting." Joe laughed.

"Aww... full of yourself huh?" Stephanie snapped back.

"Naw, just hopeful. Besides...I want you to know me first."

As Joe walked away, Stephanie hung on the door. She hated to go back in alone. She also remembered she had to call Hillary. She ran it all through her mind, and debated how to explain this all the Hill. She had always told her everything, but this was crazy. How would Hillary ever believe her? Maybe this was one secret she would have to sit on for now.

"So, you do remember me. The woman who has been by your side for all these many years. The one who listens to your every whine and complaint. Yet, gets forgotten at the very thought of a vacation where guys walk around without their shirts on. You know, big muscly tanned Adonis's who just want to work up a sweat for you. ... Guys who are probably half naked, right now in the yard in front of you. I hate you! You know that, don't you? Your phone has a camera, right?" She rambled.

"Hill, go on a date. Call the cab guy; he really wanted to climb that mountain."

"Hey, just 'cause mama is over six feet tall, does not mean she wants to be climbed by just anyone. Besides I called, and he is busy the next couple of days."

"It's OK; we both know you can do better than the cabbie."

"So, how are things with your hot stud of a ranch hand? Are you married yet?" Hillary said sarcastically. "You better not ever get married without me there. I will be the bride's maid. I will not wait to be asked. Sweetheart, which side of the aisle will I be on?" Hillary laughed so loud Stephanie had to pull the phone from her head.

"Hill you are too demented for words. For your information, when and if I get married you will be there. I could never do anything like that without you."

"Ha ha …wedding humor. So, are things progressing at all with your ranch hand?"

"He kissed me, if that is what you mean and he pretty much saw me naked. Well, down to my underwear."

"Major progress. I am so proud of you. See all you had to do is take off your clothes and a guy appreciated your body. Maybe I will go to Times Square and get naked. Do you think it would work?"

"Only for the officer who arrests you." Stephanie insisted

"Oh God, I love a man in uniform."

"Hill don't do it. It is not worth the fine you will have to pay, or the pain when you find out he is gay or married. Let it go."

"You're right, I don't have a good track record in this department. Remember that one guy I dated for two weeks, that had the big secret and then I learned he was really a drag queen and only wanted to date me because we wore the same size and he loved my clothes."

"Yeah, I remember."

"But didn't he look lovely in my blue print dress?" They broke into laughter.

"I miss you Hill."

"I miss you too Stephanie. Now tell me what is bothering you. I can tell you are withholding from me."

"Nothing is wrong, just some weird stuff happened since I got here, but nothing I want to talk about yet." Stephanie tried to put her fears to rest. If it starts to get to me, I will let you know. By the way, did you know I could ride a horse? I didn't, but today I did and I was brilliant at it. I wish you had been here to see."

"Me too! Take video next time and email it to me, and get some shots of those ranch hands. You never know, I might just decide to head to Arizona myself one of these days. Look sweetie, I need to run if I am going to get across town to do errands. Call me soon. Love you so very much. Bye!"

"Love you too, bye."

As soon as the phone went dead, Stephanie was full of energy again. She finished eating and pulled out some new clothes that weren't soaking wet and pulled on her boots. She couldn't stay cooped up waiting for whatever was going to happen. She didn't know what she was going to do, but the answers she wanted had to lie in that abandoned ghost town. That had to be where she would start. Stephanie threw a few things together that she might need, like water and a flashlight, and headed down to the stable. She had to get a horse, and get out without Joe riding along behind her.

As she walked into the stable, Stephanie looked for Joe, who was nowhere to be found. Another man was working there; it must have been time for Joe's break. Stephanie asked him for a horse and was saddled up in no time. In just a few minutes, she was out the doors and on her way past the corral. Once again, she had mounted the horse like she had been doing it her whole life. No one in her family has ever owned a horse, and until then she had no interest in them, so the whole idea that she had this hidden ability was so strange.

Stephanie stayed with the route she had taken before, when she and Joe had gone out. The sun was hotter than ever since it was the later part of the day. Stephanie wished it would rain, just cool it down a little. But there was little chance of that happening. There wasn't a cloud in the sky and from the looks of the area, there was hardly any rainfall on a regular basis.

Sweat was dripping down Stephanie's back as she reached the entrance to the valley. She slowed down long enough to take off her outer shirt and use it to wipe her face. She wasn't used to this kind of humidity and temperature. She drank a little from her bottle, and tried to make sure to keep some for later as she would probably need it on the way back.

Taking it slowly, she started the horse moving into the valley and towards the ghost town. Millions of things ran through her mind like 'how crazy she was to believe in any of this' and 'what was she thinking to be showing up on the ghost's territory'. It was too late to turn back now. She had come all the way to the town and she believed the best way to put all this to rest was to face her fear.

Just at the edge of the town she dismounted the horse and led it in beside her as she looked around. It was scarier by herself, than when she had Joe there to back her up. She found a shaded place on a side area to tie up the horse, so it was out of the sun. Hoping it was safe, she walked through the streets studying each building. Many of them were holding up to age and weather. She wondered why people would abandon a whole town and move away. Maybe it was just too remote an area for the town to survive. Bigger towns probably came in and attracted the people away.

As Stephanie walked down the side street, she saw it again, the stable area. She gazed at it intensely. The image of the building was in her memories, somewhere. She knew she had never been there before, but for some reason she knew what the stable looked like. The whole thing seemed insane. One thing was certain, she wasn't going to find any answers there.

Stephanie walked over to the house where she had seen the shadow before. It was different now. Not so threatening and no shadow to be seen. 'Maybe the ghost was at the sister's house again,' she thought to herself. Wherever he was, Stephanie was not going to sit around and wait for him. She wanted to see what was in the old house. She walked up onto the porch and it seemed solid, as did much of the interior. Going from room to room she looked for anything that might have been an indication of who had lived there. The place had been empty for so long, there was nothing left.

Stephanie was just about to give up hope, when she saw there was one door she had not tried. As she walked towards it, the floorboards started to creak and make a loud sagging noise. She turned to run for safety in the other part of the room, but it was too late. The floor came apart under her feet. A section of the wood went down to the basement with her on top of it. Stephanie didn't even have time to think as she plummeted down.

In the basement, as the floorboards crashed onto the surface, Stephanie was slammed down on her side and her head struck against a section of wall. She lay there for more than an hour before she blinked her eyes, and she reached a hand to her head. The light was dim in there, but she could tell she was bleeding and it had dripped down the side of her cheek.

Stephanie tried to stand up but was wobbly. She didn't feel like she had a concussion, but she wasn't sure. She felt around the floor, to see if she could find her flashlight, but in all the rubble she could not. She quickly realized that searching the place on her own was a mistake. As she tried again to push herself up, she felt the shirt that was tucked into her back pocket. Pulling it out, she wiped her face and tried to apply pressure to the bleeding. She was able to move a bit and stand up. As her foot drug over the floor, she heard something strange. Something metal was under her boot.

Stephanie reached down, trying to get ahold of the metal hoping it was not a nail she was about to step on. When she got it in her hand, she knew it was not a nail. It was round, …a ring, had to be. She moved around a bit more and kicked her flashlight. Turning it on she was able to see more of the situation. It was a ring she had found…a woman's ring. She thought it was strange of the ring to be in the basement of a house. She looked at the ring hard, it was slightly familiar. She had seen one before that looked like it, but she could not place where.

As Stephanie moved to look for a way out, she heard a sound. It was like someone breathing, but there was no one else there. Fear started to fill her, she wanted out now. The sound of her heart beating filled her ears and her lungs hurt as she breathed. She shined the light around the back of the room and saw what looked like the shadow of a man. It had to be the same one that was there before.

As she turned to move away, her light went out and she tripped over some piles of floorboard. She was fighting for consciousness, when she heard the man's voice. "Stephanie, are you alright? Sweetheart, you are so clumsy. One of these days you are going to break your neck."

As Stephanie looked up, there was light in the basement. She raised her head to see the beautiful dark eyes and black wavy hair of a man, who she swore she knew. The man lifted her up and held her from falling. "Look ... You dropped your ring again. We are going to have to put string on this or something, you are always losing this. If you don't want to be my woman, you don't have to wear it you know." The man spoke. Stephanie looked up as the ring was slid onto her finger. "There, just where it's supposed to be."

Stephanie wobbled around a bit as everything around her changed. She looked down and her clothes had changed and she was now wearing a dress. Her boots were different, and the room looked clean and the floorboard pieces were missing. She looked up and there was no hole in the floor. The handsome man walked her upstairs, to a fully furnished house that was clean and lived in, not dusty and abandoned. Stephanie thought to herself, 'What the hell is going on here? This has to be a dream; I am in the basement and knocked out.'

The man looked deep into Stephanie's eyes. "You want to go over to the Doc's office and get checked out?

You don't look so good. Stephanie can you hear me, my love it is me, Chance." Stephanie looked up and recognized the face; it was the same one from the picture at the ranch. Fear gripped her; she was paralyzed. "I'm Ok," she said quietly. "I just need some air is all." Chance leaned over and wrapped his arms around Stephanie and helped her walk to the front porch. As they passed through the door, Stephanie looked up, it was all as she had imagined. The town was alive in colors of fresh paint and living people that looked like they were from the old west.

Stephanie jerked back in fear, she was terrified. This couldn't be real. As she turned, Chance held her in his arms and leaned down to kiss her lips. "It's all going to be OK; I am here to take care of you." Before the words could register with Stephanie, everything grew dark. The sounds around her were echoing and she felt disjointed. The colors drained as she was in total darkness again. She could feel pain shooting through her body as she faded away.

Chapter Seven: With This Ring

Stephanie felt the pulling of her body, though she didn't know where she was being pulled or why. In her mind she retraced what had happened but nothing made sense. She was in the present, then the past. Then she remembered darkness and Chance talking to her. She remembered the comforting feeling of his presence. The way his skin felt when they touched. It felt familiar and right. It felt like someone she had loved her whole life. Then she remembered the ring; the simple gold band which was a symbol of their love. Chance had given it to her when they vowed their love for each other.

Her head spun from nausea and the concussion she had suffered. There was too much going on and she was so sick feeling. Something was wrong; she knew this was not right. She had to open her eyes but just thinking about it hurt her head. Then she heard a voice again. "It's all going to be OK; I am here to take care of you." She knew this voice. It was familiar and she tried so hard to respond. As her mouth moved, she was able to say one word… "Chance." "Stephanie, you need to wake up. You have a concussion and you can't be asleep during this."

Stephanie fought hard to make her eyes open, and when they did, she looked up to her savior. A shadow fell across his face and it was hard to see his features. As Stephanie sat up again, she tried to speak, "Chance." "What, who is Chance? It is me Joe." Stephanie leaned into Joe, as he held her in his arms. During the time Stephanie was unconscious Joe had found his way to the basement and brought her up to the front porch and tried to clean her up.

"How did you find me?" Stephanie asked.

"Wasn't hard to figure out where you had gone. I asked Mark if he had seen you, and he told me of how you took off towards the desert. I knew then exactly where you were going. You could have killed yourself coming out here alone."

"I know, I did a pretty good job of it. God, I feel as sick as a dog."

"It's the concussion. You were out for a while, and that is bad. How long had you been down there?" Joe asked.

"I don't think long, but Joe, something really weird happened. I saw this town alive again. Like back in the old west and people were here. He was here."

"What do you mean 'he' was here?"

"Chance, the man from the picture. The one I was photographed with, the man I was in a relationship with in the old west."

"Stephanie, you were not in the old west." Joe snapped.

"Then why do I remember him now, and why do I know so much about this place?"

"You banged your head really hard; it had to have something to do with that." Joe rationalized.

Stephanie closed her eyes for a moment. She knew this was one argument she was not going to win, and she was in no condition to debate the whole issue. As Stephanie opened her eyes again, she saw Joe staring at her. There was such love in his eyes and a fear of what was happening. "We have to get you home now, so we can clean you up and bandage your head." Joe brought both horses over, and tied a rope between his and Stephanie's. "Now I am going to stand you up and walk you to the horse. I need you to just hold on to me, and I should be able to get us both up."

Joe leaned Stephanie against the side of the horse, then hoisted her up. Stephanie was able to hold on long enough for Joe to come up behind her. Joe wrapped his arms around Stephanie to hold her tight, as they began their slow trot back to the ranch. Stephanie felt every bounce of the horse, but did not complain. She had done this to herself. She felt dumb for trying to go off and face down this ghost on her own. Now she had the battle wounds to prove it.

The trip seemed to take forever, and Joe tried in every way to comfort Stephanie. Holding her there on the horse, Joe knew he was falling in love. He wasn't the type to show feelings. In the past, he had always been the one to leave a relationship before it got too deep. This was the first time he didn't want to run. Holding Stephanie, felt like the most right thing he had ever done in his life. He wanted to protect her. Joe just didn't know how.

As they rode Stephanie tried to keep her eyes open. She looked around trying to place in her head how far they had come, and how much longer she would have to stay on the horse, before she could throw up. Stephanie looked down at her shirt which was covered in blood.

"I made a mess of this."

"We all make bad decisions sometimes." Joe responded.

"No, I mean my shirt. It is ruined."

"You are sick as a dog and all you are worried about is your shirt. I had to use it to stop your bleeding and clean up your head a bit. Don't worry, we will get you another shirt. I am just so thankful you didn't do more damage and I will be able to get you home again."

"Yeah, you are my hero. I like having a hero, I never had one before. No one to defend me or save me, well except Hill. She is my family, best friend, everything rolled into one. I'm glad I have you now too. She's going to kill me when she finds out." Stephanie insisted.

"You don't need to be worrying about that right now. When you are back safe and cleaned up, you can call her and let her know what has happened. Until then just take it easy."

As they moved along, the sun had already gone down and the heat was tolerable. Stephanie sat up more as they went along, and she felt the fog that covered her brain was lifting a bit. She was able to think more clearly. As she sat up, she leaned back into Joe's chest. Stephanie liked the way it felt to have Joe behind her, holding her. She could feel all the muscles of Joe's arms enveloping her. For a moment she felt protected. For once in her life, she didn't have to be in complete control and she liked this new feeling.

They arrived at the ranch late into the evening. Joe rode up to the front porch, where he found Mona waiting like a fearful mother looking for one of her children. She ran to the horse almost in tears, and she helped Joe get Stephanie down and sit her on the steps.

"Oh my god, what have you done to yourself?" She cried out.

"I am OK, don't get upset." Stephanie tried to comfort her.

"She has a concussion and a cut on her head. She bled a lot, but it has stopped now. We need to get her cleaned up and get some medicine on her wound." Joe insisted.

Mona went inside and gathered medical supplies, water and towels. When she returned, Joe had already put the horses away and was holding Stephanie. Mona looked down at them as she walked across the porch. Although the situation scared her, the love she saw between them made her heart full. She put down all the supplies and the two of them set out to clean Stephanie's wounds. Beside the house was an outdoor shower, for when the men got too dirty to come inside. The two of them held tight to Stephanie as the water blasted down her head, and a pool of red ran down to her feet.

Pulling her from the water, Stephanie looked much more alive. She was clear and her eyes were wide open. She looked at the both of them and smiled. "There's my girl!" Mona shouted. They guided Stephanie over to the steps and toweled her off. There had been more blood than damage. The cut on her head wasn't too bad and they applied medicine and bandaged it. Other than cuts and scrapes, she had emerged better than anyone had imagined. As Joe ran inside to get some clean dry clothes, Mona and Stephanie sat together on the steps.

"You know, you scared the hell out of me. And I am not easily scared."

"I'm sorry, but after what has happened and what the sisters said I felt like I had to take this on head first." Stephanie answered.

"You know you are not alone here. Whatever is going on, we will help you." Mona insisted.

"It's more than you know."

"I know everything; Miss Elizabeth and Miss Mary paid me a visit, shortly after you left them. I can't say I believe everything they say. It all sounds crazy, but we will help you through this. They said the anniversary is coming. That is just a couple of days away. During that time, we will make sure you are never alone."

Stephanie reached out and took her hand. She appreciated the love. People in the city weren't like this. No one went out of their way to help anyone. This was a welcome change to what she was used to. She smiled at her and as Stephanie pulled her hand back, Mona reached back towards her and held on.

"I never noticed you had a ring on before. Are you married? If you are, I think you are about to break Joe's heart." She remarked.

"I'm not married, I never have been." Stephanie said looking down at the ring.

"Then where did you get the ring?" Joe chimed in.

Stephanie looked hard at the ring and it all came flooding back to her. She told the story to them both of how she fell through the floor-boards and when she woke up in the past. Chance had put the ring on her hand. Stephanie quickly slid the ring off. She laid it down on the porch. She stared at it not knowing what to say or do.

"Get rid of it." Joe insisted.

"Joe, you need to calm down. We don't know what it means yet and until we do, Stephanie probably needs to hang onto it." Mona said in a protecting way. "Just don't put it on."

"I agree," Stephanie added.

"We need to get you dressed and get some water into you, so you don't dehydrate." Mona said in a mothering tone. "Joe, I'll leave the clothes to you, and I will get her something to drink and eat."

As Mona went inside Joe moved down beside Stephanie. He laid down the clothes and positioned himself on the steps looking straight into Stephanie's eyes. "I need to shine a light in your eyes to test how much of a concussion you have. This'll probably hurt your head a bit but it is necessary." Joe shined the light and Stephanie's eyes reacted. She had a mild concussion, and this would mean she had to be monitored the rest of the night while she healed.

"Yeah, I will have to check you every 30 minutes for the rest of the night, to make sure you are getting better. Good news is it could have been far worse."

"If it feels this bad like this, I don't want to know what worse is like." Stephanie moaned.

"You are going to be Ok, and the best thing is I get to spend the whole night with you."

"This is not how I would have liked our first night together to have been." Stephanie joked.

"Hey, sick or not, I don't care. I am just glad I found you and you are here with me again."

"You really do like me, don't you?"

"Yeah, I do. Can't say I have ever felt like this before or taken to anyone so fast. I don't want to fight it though. It just feels right." Joe smiled.

"So, tell me this…what happens in a couple of days when I have to face down a ghost and survive my destiny? And if I do survive, one day I have to go home, right?"

Stephanie looked down realizing everything in life isn't perfect.

"Not everything in life is easy. Caring about you is. We will deal with life as it comes. Sometimes the solution is easy. If we are in love with each other, then we find a way to stay together, either here or in the city."

"You wouldn't last a day in the city!" Stephanie said sarcastically.

'A few days ago, I would have said you wouldn't last a day here. But you are still here, bruises and all. Don't ever underestimate the power of people or love. Now, this will sound kinda rude, but I want to get you naked."

Stephanie looked at him in a half crazed and half sexual way. She knew what Joe meant. The blood soaked and dirty ripped clothes, had to come off. Joe led Stephanie to a private place beside the house and helped her strip off. As the pieces of clothing were removed, Joe tried to not look at Stephanie's naked body but he could not help himself. His eyes scanned every inch. He found Stephanie to be beautiful. This was not at all what he had expected and Joe knew he wanted her. His hormones raced as he took a deep breath. Joe tried to turn away but he couldn't.

"What's wrong? You are looking at me weird." Stephanie asked.

"Nothing's wrong. I am trying not to stare, but I can't help myself." Joe replied.

"So, you like what you see."

"Umm ... yes. You could say that. If you weren't sick right now, things might be going in a different direction."

"Aww, does Joey like me that much?" Stephanie teased him.

"Yes, and you will probably never hear me say this again in all the days we are together, but please put your clothes on." Joe laughed.

Stephanie accommodated him, trying not to laugh as she got dressed. She held back as much as she could, but every time she laughed, her head felt as if it were being pounded. Stephanie did a pretty good job moving about and putting on clothes but bending over to put on shoes was out of the question, Joe had to help her.

"You did that pretty well." Stephanie said picking at him.

"Good practice for when we have kids." Joe laughed at her.

"You want kids too?" Stephanie asked.

"Yes, I do. You would make a great mom." Joe replied.

"I think you would make a great dad." Stephanie said smiling at him.

Joe led Stephanie inside and sat her down in the dining room. Mona was there ready with food and prepared to care for her. As Stephanie ate, Joe wandered into the lobby looking at the fireplace. The pictures were still there. He studied the one with the man and woman. The couple had their arms around each other, and you could see their hands. The blond woman who looked like Stephanie was very clear in the image. You could see her left hand. On it, was a wedding ring. The image was too fuzzy to make out details but there was no denying the ring on her hand looked very much like the one Stephanie was wearing.

Joe looked at the way the woman held herself and the clothes she was wearing. It all seemed out of place with the rest of the image. This woman was not from the old west, she looked too modern. Joe put his finger to the picture as if to hide the hair and looked again. He knew it was Stephanie. The look in her eyes was the same. There was no mistaking it.

Joe's heart sank for a moment. How could this be real? Is it possible that Stephanie slipped back in time like she said she did? If so, was it going to happen again? Joe's heart raced; he couldn't lose Stephanie this way. He was just starting to warm up to the idea of loving another person. He didn't want this feeling to end.

Joe went back in, as they were finishing with the food. Stephanie looked much more alert now. She was returning to normal. Joe walked over to her and stood behind her chair. Leaning down he wrapped his arms around Stephanie and kissed her on the side of her head. Stephanie leaned back and held on; she had always wanted this feeling but never found the right person. Mona beamed at the both of them; she could not contain her joy.

"Looks like my kids are in love. It's beautiful." Mona spoke with pride.

"Yeah it is beautiful, now we just have to fight to keep it." Joe responded.

Joe and Stephanie headed upstairs. Stephanie knew she had to let Hillary know what had happened. There was too much going on, to leave her out of it. Hillary would kill her, if anything happened and she could not be there.

She dialed the phone and her heart was overwhelmed the minute she heard Hillary's voice.

"Are you sitting down?" Stephanie asked her.

"It is never good when you begin a conversation like that. Bad news first." Hillary insisted.

Stephanie told her the whole sorted story, from the pictures, to the legend, all the way down to the Ballin sisters and the trip through the floor-boards. And then there was silence. "I can get a flight out there tomorrow." Stephanie reassured her that she would be ok and that she didn't have to. Hillary didn't hear anything she had to say. Her mind was set.

"As soon as I get off this phone, I am booking a flight. No throwback ghost from the old west is going to hurt my family. Mama is on her way."

"Hill, calm down. What about Samantha? You can't leave her." She insisted.

"Oh please, we made peace, she and I get along now. I'll just tell her we are going on a mission together. She'll like that. She is good at stalking."

"You really need to think about this." Stephanie pleaded with her.

"No, I don't, if you believe this is real and it is happening, then I need to be there and help you."

Stephanie assured her it was real, and then she told her about the ring and how when she came to, it was on her finger. Hillary told her to get off the phone, she had plans to make, her mind was made up. She immediately started searching for flights and found one for the next morning. She quickly gathered things for her flight and packed everything she would need including kitty litter. Samantha clung to her side, as if she knew from the tone of Hillary's voice this was serious.

"Look Miss Kitty, we are going on a trip tomorrow. I know you are not used to this, but we have to save Mommy's firm little butt. I know you are not going to like the plane, but I will try to make this as easy on you as I can. Just pretend we are going on safari. It'll be an adventure." Samantha looked at Hillary as if she had gone crazy. Crazy or not, the trip was happening. Hillary was heading to the desert.

Chapter Eight: Hillary Goes on Safari

7 A.M. came quickly for Hillary. She was up most of the night packing and getting just the right look together for her trip. She had all her bags together when she called the cab company. She couldn't miss her plane, and needed someone she knew would show up. "I don't believe I am doing this. I need a cab, is Hank working?" She said as she looked down at the phone number and name Stephanie had told her. "Are you there God, it's me Hillary. Sounds like a bad book about my period." She laughed. "Look I have to get there and save Stephanie. Please, a little help would be appreciated."

Hillary put all her bags by the door getting ready to leave. The last thing...getting Samantha to cooperate.

That might be easier said than done, the cat was not cooperative at the best of times. As Hillary opened the carrier bag, Samantha saw her. The cat's expression was priceless and almost animated. Samantha looked at her to say, "No way in hell." And she was off on a mad dash to find any hiding place that Hillary could not fit. It was a comedy routine as Samantha ran from room to room with Hillary right on her heels…just out of reach. By the time they had been in every room in the apartment, Hillary was totally out of breath and done with the chase. "You like hiding in closets don't you, Daddy said so." Hillary opened the door, and in the cat ran.

Hillary maneuvered the cat carrier right in front of the door and in her deepest voice ordered the cat in the box. Surprisingly Samantha cooperated. "And this, is why I don't keep pets." Hillary added in a grumbly voice. She placed the carrier with all her other bags just outside the door, as Hank came down the hall looking for her. "I thought I was supposed to meet you at the curb?" She asked. "For you, pretty lady, I would worship you. I would carry bags." And he did and loaded her in the car and they were on their way to the airport.

Hillary made her flight in record time, and was one of the first ready to board the plane. She checked her luggage and then, came time to deal with Samantha. She looked the attendant straight in the eyes and unloaded the biggest lie she had ever told. "Look, long story short the cat is my emotional companion. I cannot fly without her, or I will have a massive breakdown. I need her in my lap." Surprisingly the attendant bought the story. "You are one lucky kitty; I saw someone use something similar to take their dog shopping. Remember this, the next time you feel like being a pain in the ass. I could have just thrown you in the cargo hold." Hillary made a superiority face after her read of the situation, and headed to her seat on the flight.

~~~~~

Stephanie made it through the night with Joe at her side. Somewhere around 5A.M. they checked Stephanie's eyes again, and she was normal. She crashed shortly after from exhaustion. She lay on the bed for just a few minutes and was out cold. Joe was exhausted as well and tried to stay awake, but ended up curled behind, wrapping his arms around Stephanie. They slept for hours, until Stephanie began to dream. She was with Chance again. The dream was more of a nightmare, being she didn't know how to get home. She was stuck in the past. She wanted to get home to Joe, but didn't know how to break free. She thrashed back and forth and called out Joe's name. Joe woke up frightened by the noise Stephanie was making.

"Stephanie, wake up I am here."

"What, what happened?" Stephanie asked.

"You were dreaming. You called out my name like you were scared." Joe answered her.

"I was there again, in the past. I was trying to come home, but I didn't know how."

"It's alright, it's all a dream, you are OK and I am here to take care of you."

Stephanie was comforted by the idea the Joe was there. She leaned back into the pillow, and they lay there looking into each other's eyes. Stephanie lifted her hand and ran her finger around the edge of Joe's face and caressed him gently. Joe looked up at her with his sexy bedroom eyes, working up the nerve, he took Stephanie in his arms and held her tight. "If I am wrong, tell me to stop. Stephanie did not stop him and positioned herself in a way the Joe could climb on top of her. They kissed deep and hard. Stephanie liked the feeling of being taken. She had always desired it. In her mind, she thought there was something familiar about it.

As they kissed and rolled, Stephanie's left hand moved above Joe and she could see the ring. She was sure she had taken it off. The night before, she had placed it on the nightstand. As she stared at the ring, things changed, she wasn't at Mona's anymore. It was a bedroom of a strange house. This was the ghost town. She remembered being there. It was as if she was living the life of the Stephanie from that time. Stephanie pulled back for a second and realized more had changed; she wasn't kissing Joe anymore. Chance had replaced him.

As Stephanie pulled back away from his embrace, Chance sat back on the bed. His long muscular body was tight. With every movement his muscles flexed and hardened. He stood up totally naked and walked to the window to open it. "It's getting hot in here. Or maybe you are just making me that way." Chance laughed. He turned back, and Stephanie could see every inch that swung between his legs. He climbed back into bed on top of her. "I want you. I need to be with you now." He said sliding Stephanie's underwear off. Stephanie leaned back in fear not knowing what to do. This was someone else's life. She put her hands over her eyes and recoiled as she felt Chance spreading her legs.

"Hey are you alright? If I am going too fast, I can slow down. I know you banged your head and it probably still hurts. Stephanie can you hear me." Joe reached out to touch her, just as Stephanie looked up and realized she was back where she belonged. "I'm Ok; my head is kind of hurting. I'm sorry, I really want to. I want you. I just need to get my head together." Stephanie said lovingly to him. "I understand you have been through a lot. Our time will come." Joe spoke softly. "We could still be here together, naked for a while, if you can handle that?" Joe shook his head yes and crawled back in beside Stephanie under the sheet. They were closer than ever; yet in Stephanie's mind separated by a hundred years and a ghost.

Later that evening, Hillary's plane landed in Arizona. She grabbed up Samantha and headed to the door of the plane. As she pushed past other passengers, she was like a woman on a mission. She finally made her way to the front of the line and was ready to leave the plane when she felt the heat coming from outside the door. "What the hell; it is like an oven and I haven't even gotten outside." She grumbled to the woman behind her. Hillary emerged from the plane in full safari apparel, looking as if she was going into the Congo wearing khaki shorts, matching shirt and an explorer hat.

As she walked into the baggage claim, an older woman from the flight walked up to her and asked, "What are you dressed for dear." She only replied. "An adventure!" It was true, Hillary was there for an adventure, as much as saving Stephanie. In her mind, she didn't see why she couldn't have both. Before leaving the airport, she made a quick stop into the gift shop and bought two bottles of water. As she dragged her bags out into the open area, and arranged herself, Samantha started to meow. "Don't worry my girl; one of these bottles is for you. Why do you think I brought an empty bowl as well?"

Hillary headed out of the airport doors and into the parking lot looking for Stephanie. She was unprepared for the intense heat. The moment she saw Stephanie and Joe, she got excited jumped up and down a couple of times and collapsed. They rushed over and gathered her up. It was a good thing she had just bought the water. In the back of the van, Hillary came around and was back to her old self as Stephanie leashed up Samantha and walked her over in the grassy area beside the parking lot. "Poor girl, I am so glad

to see you, but Hill should have never brought you here."
She said giving her a bowl of water and allowing her to
have a moment of freedom.

Once Hillary recovered, everyone was back in the
van and the air conditioning on, they headed out. Hillary
looked like a big child crammed in the back seat. The area
was not large, and she was a tall woman of six foot one
who had quite a few curves. She made due, with the
luggage crammed in, and a cat in her lap.

"Hill, I am glad you came and that you are really
concerned, but I don't know how it will help." Stephanie
spoke trying to seem grateful.

"Hmm, let's see if I got this right. You see yourself
in an old west photo. Two little old ladies say it is you, and
you are about to celebrate the anniversary of your death
possibly by dying. Then you go to the old west ghost town,
see a ghost that takes you back in time to give you a
wedding ring, which I notice you currently still possess by
the way. And you get your head bashed, have a concussion

and you look like hell. Have I missed anything?" She blasted out, her voice getting louder and louder. "You, most definitely, need all the help you can get!"

Stephanie looked back at her. She knew when Hillary raised her voice, she meant business and that she had just wounded her. The expression on her face changed, as she looked into Hillary's eyes. She went from standoffish, to goofy and loving in one quick move. Stephanie could never win with Hillary and she knew it. They loved each other too much. Since they met, they had been family. Hillary once told her that you can't always choose your biological family, and they may not always be there. But sometimes in life, you get that rare opportunity to create a family, from the people you know and those bonds can sometimes be the strongest. Stephanie knew she was lucky to have her.

"What do we do now?" Stephanie asked as she leaned back into her seat.

"I say we go find this ghost and kick his ass." Hillary blasted back.

"Can I be a part of this conversation?" Joe asked.

"Yes, of course." they both answered him at the same time.

"I don't know what we will accomplish by pissing off the ghost who can take Stephanie out of time and drag her to the old west. We have to be careful and keep Stephanie out of Chance's path until the anniversary is over with."

"And what if we can't?" Stephanie asked. "What if he comes for me and you cannot stop him?"

"We will stop him some way." Hillary tried to comfort Stephanie by putting her hand on her shoulder.

"Look, all I know is, that there are pictures on the fireplace that show me in the old west."

"So, what about them?" Joe asked.

"Well, if they exist, then it means at some point I will be going back in time again. I looked at the pictures and I thought about it. The woman in those photos has to be me. And since I have already been there once and we know it is possible for Chance to drag me there, it might just happen again. I just need a way to get back, if it happens."

"What happened before you went back last time? Did anything happen to make you go there?" Hillary asked.

Stephanie ran it all through her head again. How she saw the shadow and then how it became a man. She fell through the floor-boards and then found the ring. The ring had to have something to do with it. "It was the ring. It is the link to the past; he needs to pull me back. When I was with him and wearing it, I felt like I belonged there and the memories of the place were mine."

"So, you are saying there may well have been another Stephanie. But in the pictures, it is you?" Joe tried to make since of it.

"He thinks I am the reincarnation or whatever of his Stephanie. By dragging me back he thinks I can just take over where the original Stephanie left off. It's the only thing that makes sense."

"How did the original Stephanie die?" Hillary asked.

"I don't know, the Ballin sisters never told me all that. I had to get away from them, they scared me." Stephanie laughed.

"Well I see another visit with the sisters happening tomorrow. But this time you have backup. I have lived in New York my whole life. I have seen it all, I was there for 9/11, I was there for a couple of bad-assed hurricanes, I was there for the corona virus, and I was even there for Harold and Maude on Broadway. Trust me; the last one was the scariest of all. So, if they think they can scare me with crazy, they have another thing coming. They want crazy, I got their crazy." Hillary smirked with an insane look on her face.

Stephanie looked back at her as if she had lost it. But in truth she did feel safe with her there. Maybe she was just a hint of her familiar life that she needed. She couldn't help but feel bad for Samantha as she was trapped in Hillary's arms and could not escape. The cat, wearing a small safari hat, looked terrified and just as insane as Hillary did. Stephanie smiled at them, knowing how lucky she was, and then turned to Joe. He had become the latest member of this growing family of lunatics.

Chapter Nine: Tea and Cakes with a Crazy Woman Named Hillary

The next morning before Stephanie could crawl out of bed, she heard a noise from outside her door. It was a constant creaking. There was someone or something right outside her door, moving back and forth. Fear overtook her, as her mind raced through all kinds of scenarios. Back and forth the sound traveled, and she knew the sound now, it was creaking floor boards. 'Do ghosts creak floorboards?' She thought to herself. She was sure they did not, and worked up the nerve to go to the door and open it. As she flung it open, there stood Hillary.

"Hill, what the hell are you doing out here? You scared me to death."

"Oh, did I disturb you?" She said sarcastically. "I am only here to protect you."

"Yeah, that much I know, but the way you were outside the door. I thought you might have been our friend the ghost." Stephanie snapped.

"Well, if I were the ghost, which obviously I am not, I would not even use a door, thank-you very much"

"Ok, point taken." Stephanie admitted in defeat. "How long have you been here anyway?" She asked.

"Long enough to hear you having a nightmare about Casper."

"Who is Casper? Oh, I get it, that is smart ass for Chance."

"You can call him anything you want, as long as we get through today and he is out of your life forever." Hillary was done with the conversation. "When do we have tea and cakes with the Ballin sisters?"

"Mona called for us, and they said any time we wanted to stop by this morning was fine."

"Good, I have already taken care of the cat; I gave her food, water and assembled her kitty cat condo. Let's go."

"Hill, when did Samantha get a kitty cat condo?" Stephanie had no idea what she was talking about.

"Cat's gotta have a place to cut loose. I came prepared."

They met Joe outside. He had expected they would be ready early. Hillary was wasting no time; she was like a mother hen. Nothing was hurting Stephanie, not on her watch. As they pulled down the drive, Joe was eerily silent. Stephanie glanced at him several times as they headed out of the property. She wanted to speak so badly, but fear was taking her over. Why all of a sudden was Joe acting so weird? As Stephanie glanced back at Hillary, she slapped her in the back of the shoulder as if to tell her to do something.

"Joe, why are you so quiet, did something happen?" Stephanie asked.

"No, I'm just a little uneasy. I was up most of the night, running this through my brain. I just don't understand how this can be happening." Joe responded.

"Oh, for a minute I thought I did something wrong." Stephanie breathed a sigh of relief.

"No, you didn't do anything. I just don't know how to fight the undead. How can you fight something you don't understand and who has all the power?"

"I don't know, but I will do whatever it takes to stay here with you two. I am not going down without a fight." Stephanie said with a feeling of confidence.

They pulled up to the driveway of the sister's house. As the van rounded the corner, Joe stopped. They all looked forward and took a deep breath at the same time. Ready or not, they had arrived and there was no going back. As Joe let up on the brake, the car rolled slowly down the drive until they came to the front porch.

Hillary stepped out first like a commando and started surveying the area. She had no idea what she was looking for. Before her was just a really old house suitable for a couple of old women. She just couldn't find anything wrong with that. Stephanie and Joe joined her and together they walked towards the front door. As Stephanie opened the screen door to knock, the inner door flung open.

"So, you are finally here? I was wondering what took you so long." Miss Elizabeth snapped.

"Wow, what a bitch." Hillary replied under her breath.

"What was that dear?" Miss Elizabeth said sternly.

"Oh, um nothing, what a nice house you have." Hillary lowered her eyes like a child being scorned.

Miss Mary entered the room just as they were all sitting down. "It is so nice to see you all. Stephanie you look well." She said as if she expected her to be dead already.

"I am fine Miss Mary. These are my friends, Joe and Hillary. They came with me to hear more about the ghost."

"Oh, you mean Chance. He has been here again since you last were." Miss Elizabeth grumbled.

"Did he come for tea and cakes as well?" Hillary couldn't resist.

"Ah, rudeness, we don't do that here in Arizona. We have manners." Miss Elizabeth retaliated.

"Well, I am from New York, and we do." Hillary said proudly.

"Why, I never…" Miss Elizabeth pulled back being put in her place.

"Did you used to be a nun, I went to Catholic school, and I had a teacher very much like you." Hillary couldn't resist one last jab.

"Ladies, let's all calm down." Stephanie insisted.

There was no stopping Hillary and Miss Elizabeth. The two were an even match. It seemed as though no one had ever challenged Miss Elizabeth before, and Hillary was determined to win. Stephanie turned to Hillary and attempted to stare her down, but it did not work. As the two women were about to go into round two, the unthinkable happened. Miss Mary, who appeared to be the most loveable quiet woman on earth, got angry.

Miss Mary stood up and walked over to the fireplace. She turned to look at the both of them. After quietly clearing her throat, she opened her mouth and let loose with the most bone chilling yell they had ever heard.

"Look here sister, you need to sit down and shut up and quit upsetting our guests. It is un-lady like to show such bad manners to a guest. Papa would be mortified by you. I know you have a mean streak, and I have lived with it for all these years, but today I am finished." Miss Mary took control like she never had before.

"Yeah, you tell her." Hillary interjected.

"Quiet Miss, I will get to you in a minute when I have finished saying my piece to my sister. Now sister, you may be older than me, but that does not make you right all the time. And right now, is not a time to be arguing, this girl is in trouble, and we have to do what we can to help her."

Then Miss Mary turned to Hillary. "My dear where I come from, you don't enter someone's house and make trouble. I don't care where you come from. So, while you are in my house, you will behave. Understand!" As she finished the last word, Miss Mary looked at Hillary in a way similar to an ax murderer who was sizing up her prey.

"I am sorry Miss Mary. I did not mean to upset you." Hillary spoke up.

The expression on Miss Mary's face changed completely looking like a sweet old lady again. "Tea my dear?" She asked.

Stephanie and Joe leaned back into the couch, in fear of what they just witnessed. Maybe Miss Elizabeth wasn't the evil one after all. At that point, no one wanted to take on either one of them.

"Can you tell us anything more about Chance or what is about to happen?" Stephanie asked.

"Like we said, he's been back. Just yesterday it was. Same old thing... out in the garden walking around. Like he is looking for something or someone." Miss Elizabeth commented.

"He knows it is the anniversary. He wants you my dear. You can hear his wails and moans, like he is heartbroken. His Stephanie has been gone so long. He wants to recreate what he has lost, and you are his love born again." Miss Mary shook her head.

"How did his Stephanie die?" Hillary said accepting cake from Miss Elizabeth.

"No one knows. She was there one day and then gone the next." Miss Mary answered.

Hillary made an odd face, like she had just put another piece in the puzzle. "And Chance died how?"

"He was killed in a fire. The barn burned down on the ranch where he worked. Just so happens the barn was in our back yard. It was long before Papa bought the land. Our garden is over most of the area the barn was, or so we are told." Miss Mary chimed in.

"Strange thing was, he died in the fire, but he could have gotten out. Maybe he wanted to die. Stephanie was gone and maybe he lost his will to live. I don't know. Something just wasn't right about the story we heard." Miss Elizabeth said sitting down in the chair beside Hillary.

As Hillary looked up at Miss Elizabeth, they seemed to find a peaceful place between them. Perhaps in some ways they were more alike than different. Hillary reached out her hand to touch Miss Elizabeth. Peace had been reached. Miss Elizabeth smiled in an awkward way, as if she did not do it often, but the meaning was sincere.

"So, we have a ring that could trap you in the past, and a ghost who is willing to drag you there to replace the Stephanie of that time. It is safe to say you should not put on the ring under any circumstances." Joe insisted. "He wants you to wear it. Maybe, that seals your fate."

"I agree." Stephanie answered. "There is just something about the way Chance died that isn't right with me and the fact that Stephanie's death has just been forgotten."

"Maybe she didn't die." Miss Elizabeth insisted.

"What do you mean?" Hillary asked.

"What if she didn't die before Chance? She wasn't in the fire, that we know of. Maybe she went on to live a long life. Perhaps, that is why there was no record of it." Miss Elizabeth answered.

"Yeah, but do I live a long life in the past or present? Stephanie asked.

Just as Stephanie asked her question, the sounds from the garden started up. Stephanie and the others made their way out the front door and around the side of the house. It was there in the center of the garden they saw the dark swirling mass. It started out small and then grew in size. As it grew, the sounds coming from within, grew as well. The sounds were of anguish and torment. It sounded as if a person were being tortured. The sisters were the first to move out into the open. A look of sadness ran across both their faces as they looked back at Stephanie. Miss Mary had a tear running down her face as she looked at her. "Only you can stop this."

Chapter Ten: Ripped Through Time

Stephanie stepped forward and walked toward the sisters. As she moved, Joe and Hillary both grabbed her arms, trying to pull her back. Stephanie knew what she had to do. Running from the ghost was not the answer; she had to face this head on. She did not want to take a chance of the others getting hurt. She turned to Hillary, "I'm going to be alright. I love you so much. Just take care of yourself and Samantha if anything happens."

"I love you too, and I will take care of her. Just promise me, whatever happens, you will come back to me." Hillary pleaded as tears ran down her face.

"I will, and you know I have never broken my word to you."

"Yeah, but you were never abducted by the living dead before." She laughed.

"Joe, we only just met and you have stood by me more than my real family has. I will find my way back to you, no matter what happens. You are everything I ever wanted. I will not let go of what is happening between us."

"Oh god, I don't want this to happen. I'm falling in love with you. I just don't know what to do." Joe said as he threw his arms around Stephanie.

"Just keep loving me. I'm going to come back to you. I promise."

As Stephanie turned towards the black mass, her fingers pulled away from Joe. She walked slowly towards her greatest fear. She came up alongside the sisters who were watching intently to see the figure take form. As the black swirl grew, its features became clear. From the unshaped mass, the face of a man came and then the outline of his body. Within minutes it had completely taken on the appearance of Chance.

He stood there transparent but gaining form. Stephanie stopped for a moment as Miss Mary hugged her. She turned to speak to Miss Elizabeth, and before she could, the old lady threw her arms around Stephanie. She was shocked by her actions. Miss Elizabeth kissed her cheek and pulled away, realizing she had let her human side be seen.

Stephanie turned back towards Chance, and for a moment gathered her courage. She inched her way closer. Her brain was spinning from all that was happening. She knew deep inside, that she could not loose herself in all this. Her only hope was to remember who she was and where she came from.

As Chance took full form, he looked up at Stephanie with an eerie smile. He was almost demonic looking in his ghostly form. Stephanie tried to remember that this was not happening out of maliciousness, but because Chance loved his Stephanie. Problem was, the love was for another woman and another lifetime. If this was a case of reincarnation, Stephanie didn't remember that lifetime, or have the love they shared.

"Stephanie you came back. I knew you would. You couldn't desert me." Chance spoke in an echoed distant voice. He sounded much like a static radio broadcast from the past.

"I am here. What do you want from me?" Stephanie asked.

"I want you to come home with me. I want to make things right between us."

"I don't belong there. I'm not your Stephanie. I may look like her and sound like her, but she was another woman from another time."

"You are her. You just don't remember yet. Put on your ring, it will all come back to you."

Stephanie reached into her pocket and pulled out the ring. She remembered having it on before, and the life of the woman who had it before her. If she put it on, she risked losing herself. She turned and looked at all her friends gathered behind them. There was so much love for her there. Their love was strong and she was sure she could count on it to save her, no matter what the situation. The wind around the garden began to pick up like a swirl and was wrapping around them. It started to throw debris everywhere. The dust stung Stephanie's eyes as she worked up the nerve to do what she had to do. "I love you all." Were the last words from her lips as she slid the ring over her finger.

The ring worked into place with a perfect fit like it had been molded for her. Stephanie walked over to Chance and took his hand. The wind raged even harder as they made contact. A strange electricity filled the air, sparking as it touched their skin. The others looked on in disbelief, as a swirl of light started to cascade around the two of them.

Stephanie looked away from Chance, not trying to let him see the expression on her face. She was not about to let her fear show. As the light was encompassing them,

Stephanie spoke her last words. "Whatever happens, I will find a way back to you, remember that." And then they were gone, and the wind calmed down to a gentle breeze.

The sisters ushered Hillary and Joe inside and tried to comfort them as best they could. No one truly knew what any of this meant. The only thing they were sure of, was that Stephanie was taken away.

~~~~~~

Stephanie awoke from her dream. As she sat up in bed her head cleared. She wondered how long she had slept. She hated waking up and not knowing the time of day. She crawled out of bed totally naked and walked down the hall. She felt groggy and out of sorts. She had almost forgotten her way around the house. When she got down the stairs, she smelled something familiar. Chance was making her breakfast. Stephanie smiled, she hated to cook, and Chance always did it better than her.

Stephanie sneaked up behind him and wrapped her arms around Chance's stomach. Chance turned and they embraced in a kiss. Their naked bodies intertwined each other. The heat from their bodies rivaled that of the stove.

"If you keep this up, I will never get your breakfast cooked." Chance laughed.

"I could go hungry for a while, if you want to come back to bed." Stephanie teased him.

"You sure you want to do that? After the way you banged your head, I thought you would be out of commission for a few days."

"My head is fine. I don't remember." Stephanie's voice trailed off as she spoke.

A rush of pain filled her head. Something was not right, but she could not put her finger on it. She felt odd but did not know why. She went back to the bedroom and looked in the mirror. Her head was bandaged. She just didn't know why. She slowly pulled the wrapping away from her head to look underneath. When the last piece fell away, she stared in confusion. There was nothing there, no cut or bruise. There was no reason for her pain either.

Stephanie heard Chance coming up the stairs, and quickly replaced the bandages on her head. She didn't know why this was happening but she was prepared to go along with it until she could make sense of it. All she knew was that something was not right.

"Why did you go away so quickly, your food is ready?" Chance said staring at her.

"I was just tightening my bandages; they seemed a bit loose."

"You want me to help you?"

"No, I took care of it. I'm fine."

"You seem to be a little odd, you sure you don't need to go back to see the town doc again?" Chance asked.

"No, I am good, just need to take it a bit easy I guess." Stephanie smiled at him hiding her unsure feelings.

They got dressed and ate. As Chance got ready to go for the day, he couldn't help worrying about Stephanie.

He hated to leave her like this, but he knew he had to go to work in the barn.

"Come with me, you can sit and watch me do all the work. You like doing that." Chance laughed loudly.

"I'll be fine on my own. I just need to stay off my feet. Standing up is not my strong point right now."

"You know I love you, right?"

Stephanie looked up into his eyes. "Of course, I do. I love you too."

As Chance left, Stephanie walked through the door of the house and onto the porch. The bright light of the morning shined in her eyes. It was hot, dry and dusty. She was blinded for a second, as she looked out to see Chance swinging his leg up and over the horse. Chance waved as he started to ride off. Stephanie waved back. Just then an older woman walked past the front of the house.

"Hello Mrs. Chancellor. How are you today?" She asked

"I'm doing well Stephanie. How is your head? I have been worried about you, ever since I heard about your accident." She replied.

"I'm fine, just need some rest is all. Talk to you soon."

The old lady smiled as she walked on. Stephanie looked on in confusion. She knew the old woman, but did not know how she knew her. Her name came so easily, but she had no knowledge of when she had first met her or how long she had known her. She was beginning to think she really had hit her head. Maybe she did have a concussion. None of this made sense.

Back inside the house, she ran it all through her brain. She knew Chance the minute she saw him, but a lot of the memories of the two of them seemed distant and clouded. Stephanie wasn't sure of a lot of things, but what she was sure of, was that she couldn't tell anyone what was wrong. She had to keep this to herself for as long as possible. Maybe in time she could make sense of it. Just like a puzzle, she needed a few more pieces. She just didn't know where to go to look for more of the pieces. For a moment she was scared.

Mullins

Chapter Eleven: Meanwhile Back In the Present

Hillary stood there, staring out over the garden. She had been there for hours and refused to leave. Everyone was in disbelief that Stephanie left as she did without even a fight. It just didn't seem right. Joe walked up behind her and paused for a minute, not knowing what to say or do. He barely knew Hilary but, in a way, they had become friends.

"I don't know what to do." Hillary whispered not turning or looking at him.

"I know. I don't think there is anything we can do." You could hear the pain in Joe's voice.

"I have to believe Stephanie had a plan. The way she left; she knew there was a way to save herself without getting us in danger." She said looking at the ground.

For the first time Hillary took her eyes off the place where Stephanie had left from. She turned to Joe, as the tears began to roll down her face. She moved towards him and he put his arms around her. Joe tried to comfort her, but he knew the only thing that would help her now, was Stephanie returning through the rift.

Inside the house, the sisters were deep in discussion as Joe and Hillary entered. They had come up with a theory that might ease everyone's worrying if Stephanie was able to do her part.

Miss Elizabeth spoke up. "I know you two think we are just a couple of eccentric old ladies. I can live with that. But we are not stupid or simple. One thing has become clear to us. Stephanie can let us know what is going on."

"How can she do that? She's trapped in the past." Hillary said in a state of confusion.

"The pictures!" Miss Mary chimed in. "She is in pictures."

"Oh my god, we never thought of that before." Joe whispered.

"Stephanie is not stupid; she would remember that. The ones at the ranch showed Stephanie with different hair. When she left here, she was just as we knew her, if the picture has changed that means she has made it back safely." Hillary added.

"But how long will it take for the pictures to change? Could it be days, or weeks?" Miss Elizabeth asked.

"I don't know, but as soon as we know something, we will let you know." Joe said as he and Hillary headed out the door.

Joe pulled out so quickly onto the road, that he threw dust and dirt everywhere. He was a man determined to get back to the ranch. Hillary just hung on; she didn't even speak. She knew how important this was.

When they arrived back at the ranch, both ran up the steps, nearly knocking Mona out of the door way. As they arrived at the fireplace, their hopes seemed to sink. The images had not changed. Everything was as it always was.

"So, what does this mean?" Hillary asked.

"What does what mean?" Mona had no idea of what had happened.

"She's gone." Joe said with a shaky voice.

Joe explained the whole thing to Mona who was heartbroken. She had adored Stephanie since she arrived. She shook her head and wouldn't believe it. She knew in her heart Stephanie was OK and would return to them. Hillary wanted to believe her so badly, but there was this fear deep inside they had all been wrong about Stephanie being able to come back.

~~~~~~

Stephanie paced back and forth around the house. She felt so alone and confused. She didn't understand why her memory was so cloudy. She felt as if she were looking out a window into another world, one she knew about but never had experienced before.

As she walked back and forth through the living room, the creaky floorboard groaned and made awful noises. In places, she looked down and saw that there were cracks in the boards that went all the way to the cellar. She was going stir crazy and as she walked back and forth, she played with her ring. It was so loose, she wondered why it was not sized properly. As she let go of her hand, and it fell to her side, the ring slid down her finger. Before she could catch it, the ring fell to the floor and rolled to one of the wider gaps in the floor boards.

Stephanie jumped for the ring but she was too late. As she fell to the floor, she could see it sliding between the boards. She knew she had to find the ring. She thought to herself, Chance would be angry if she lost it again. Then she questioned herself as to why she would think that. She had no conscious memory of losing the ring before.

As she descended the stairs to the cellar, the room was dark and there was little to no light, except what was coming through the floorboards. As she looked around the floor, she realized this was not going to be an easy task. As she looked upwards to the floor above her; her head started to spin. There was an uneasy sick feeling building in her stomach. She felt the room start to spin as she fell to her knees.

For a moment, Stephanie held herself upright. Then she fell to her side and passed out on the floor. She lay there in the dark hole of a room, her head spinning out of control. She imagined if she had ever been an alcoholic, and came down from a bad high, it would feel like that. When she could sit up, she moved slowly and propped herself up just enough, to throw up the contents of her stomach which mostly consisted of cake.

"Why am I throwing up cake? I haven't had any … Oh my god, Miss Mary's cake." It came flooding back to her. "Miss Mary made me eat her cake before Chance brought me here. But why am I just now remembering?" As she tried to stand up, her foot hit something familiar. It was the ring.

As she bent over to pick it up, memories flooded her head again. She quickly dropped the ring into her pocket and instantly her head stopped spinning. She looked up for a second and the memory of falling through the floor above, raced through her mind. It was all too familiar. She knew that was where she found the damn ring in the first place.

"So, when you are put onto my finger, you flood me with memories that are not my own. I guess the longer I wear you, the more I become the other Stephanie." She said to herself. "Well guess what, you are staying in my pocket. I will not be controlled. Maybe if I hold on to you, and can make it back to my time, then you won't be in the cellar for a future me to find."

Stephanie climbed the stairs that led her back to day light. It seemed the longer she had the ring off, the more clear she was. She cleaned herself up and rummaged through the bedroom for other clothes to put on. She needed to get out of the house. If she was going to find a way home, she needed to know what was around her.

As she stepped out into the street, the bright light hit her eyes hard, with a stinging feeling like they were on fire. She couldn't decide if it was because the sun was that bright, or she was still suffering from her session of throwing up. One thing was clear; she would have to adjust to it, because there were no sunglasses in the old west. A fact she was painfully becoming aware of.

As she stepped down off of the front porch; several people walked by waving and saying hello to her. Many wished her well, since they knew that she had recently hurt her head. She smiled and faked friendliness toward them.

After a while it made her want to scream that they were talking to the wrong person. But she decided if they wanted to be friendly, it would probably only help her in the end, if they thought she was their Stephanie. Being from New York City, she was not used to people just walking up and being friendly, it was a bit unsettling. Usually in the city, if people were nice to you, it meant they wanted something. She decided it was a pleasant change from people just speaking to ask for money.

Stephanie walked through the town as her mind kept moving to the same subject, 'What happened to the original Stephanie?' There had to have been a Stephanie before; there were too many memories of her life there. How could the ring control someone this way? It was all too weird for her. Could the real Stephanie have died? She was obviously in some kind of accident. Stephanie needed information, but who could she ask?

Chance rounded the corner as Stephanie walked through town. He ran up to her and grabbed her arm from behind. Stephanie spun around and jerked free of him not knowing what was going on.

"Oh, it was you." Stephanie said faking a smile.

"Yeah it's me; I thought you were staying at home."

"I just needed some air, and I thought a walk would do me good." Stephanie smiled, realizing she was lying and telling the truth at the same time.

"Well, I will walk with you then. I was going to get you anyway."

"Why is that?" Stephanie asked.

"Over at the Ballin place, they bought this really expensive camera and they wanted to take a picture of all the ranch hands. Old man Ballin said you could be in the picture too."

They headed to the horse, and Chance threw himself over the horses back. He reached down and took Stephanie's hand and pulled her up behind. Stephanie wrapped her arms around Chance's waist. She held on tight as the horse began to move. The tighter she held, the more she could feel the muscles in Chance's stomach. The feeling was nice, but so wrong. Stephanie couldn't help but feel attracted to him. A part of her wanted Chance. To feel their bodies wrapped around each other, but she knew this man was a stranger to her. She just couldn't let this happen.

They arrived at the ranch, just as the group was assembling for the photos. Chance and Stephanie moved to the back of the group. Stephanie instantly recognized the line-up. This was just like in the image at the ranch. It dawned on her, if she could change the image, maybe someone in the future would notice. She ran it all through her mind; she had little time to think. Then it hit her. The Stephanie in the photo had different hair and the ring. She pulled her hair to the side in a pony tail; she just had to show her ring finger.

As the photo was about to be taken, Stephanie moved her left hand up to her head. It would be clearly shown that there was no ring. As the flash powder blew,

Stephanie knew she was successful. A smile washed over her face. Her friends would know she was for the moment safe.

Chapter Twelve: Hillary Mounts a Horse

It was late when Stephanie and Chance arrived home. Stephanie had done a good job of hiding the ring. She knew it had to be off her hand. She could not risk being taken over by the memories it possessed. As they headed up the stairs to their bedroom, Chance wrapped his strong arms around Stephanie's waist.

"You feeling alright?" Chance asked her.

"As good as could be expected. Why do you ask?"

"Because ... I want you; I need to be with you."

Stephanie's mind raced, she didn't know how she could get out of this one. It was the one thing she had not planned on. She looked at Chance studying him, trying to stall. She just couldn't come up with anything. She remembered being with Joe and seeing Chance instead. But that ghost was so different from this man. Chance seemed so loving and the ghost so desperate and evil. How could they be the same person? It just didn't make sense.

Chance took Stephanie's hand and led her to the bed. As Stephanie stood there in disbelief, Chance took off his shirt. As it slid off his arms Stephanie was captivated. His ripped muscles flexed with his every move. Stephanie couldn't help but stare, as he unbuttoned his jeans and they fell to the floor revealing his manhood. Stephanie knew there was no escaping what was about to happen. Chance turned down the bedside oil lamp as he walked over to Stephanie and slowly started to unbutton her shirt.

~~~~~~

The next morning Hillary awoke early. Samantha was having no part of sleeping in. She had left her condo early in the morning, to climb onto the bed next to Hillary. Through everything that had happened, they had bonded. Samantha totally accepted Hillary. She climbed up on

Hillary's hip and started walking back and forth. As Hillary awakened, she petted the cat, as if this had been a part of their routine all along. "Bet you want some breakfast huh? Well let's get this going because Mommy has some stuff to do today."

Hillary closed her door after making sure Samantha was safe inside. As she turned around, she saw Stephanie's door. The pain shot through her and the memory flooded back. She was gone, and she felt weak and helpless. And then she realized there was a light on in her room. She got excited and bolted for the door. Maybe she had come back. As she reached for the knob, the door swung further open.

"Oh my god, Joe! What are you doing here?" She asked.

"I spent the night in her room. I wanted to feel close to her."

"I totally get it; I wish I had thought of that. It was just me and the cat last night."

"So, what are you doing today?" Joe asked her.

"I thought we might take a tour of a ghost town." Hillary said with her eyes lighting up.

"OK, but I don't know what that will help."

They walked down the stairs together, to find Mona by the fireplace. "I think you two better look at this." They moved alongside her as she picked up the picture. Hillary ran her finger over the picture to point at Stephanie's hand.

"She's not wearing the ring. She must be OK." Hillary blurted out.

"The hair has changed as well." Joe added.

"So, we know she is alright, but how do we get her back?" Hillary smiled holding the picture close to her chest.

~~~~~~~

Stephanie awoke early. Chance was lying next to her on the bed. The sun caressed the form of his beautiful naked body. For a moment, Stephanie just looked at him.

The night before was not anything Stephanie intended or wanted to happen. In her mind, she told herself that if she was to survive this and get home, she was going to have to play the game. She had to be the other Stephanie. It did not stop the feeling of guilt that filled her heart. She wanted Joe, but when Chance lowered her onto the bed and slid down on top of her, Stephanie had no choice but to go with it.

Stephanie had never been with a man like Chance before. The two of them had sex for hours. She didn't love Chance, but there was something so familiar about their being together. There was a hunger between them, a raw savage aggression. It was like the leftover memories of the other Stephanie, reminded her how good it could feel. Stephanie felt satisfied in some disgusting way that she could not explain. She wanted to feel it again, but she knew she could not give into her wanting. The time, the place and the man were not right. She had to figure a way back.

Stephanie gently slipped out of bed. Chance was so exhausted, he never knew. As Stephanie inched her way down the creaky steps, she desperately wanted to send a message to Hillary, but how? She sat down on a chair in the kitchen and scanned the place. The only house that was in her time, and the future was the house she was in. She knew Hillary would come there eventually. It was in her nature; she would have to see the place. She just had to leave a message in a way Hillary would find it.

Her mind raced to every movie and TV show she had ever watched. And then she remembered…the old Superfriends cartoon. When Aquaman was stuck in the past, he buried his communicator in a place that it could send a signal in the future. If she hid a message in a way that could not be seen now, but would be seen in the future, Hillary would see it. She was always so nitpicky about things and had to look at them. Her obsession with cartoons was about to pay off.

On the wall of the house in the future the wallpaper was peeling. It was the same paper that was on the wall in front of her. Since no one would live in the house after Chance, there was a safe bet no one would find her message. Stephanie gently pulled at the edge of the paper and freed it in a way that it did not tear and it could be replaced. She found a pencil and wrote a quick message. 'I'm fine and in control for now. Just need to find the original Stephanie. Maybe then I can get home.'

She then pressed the edge of the wallpaper back to its trim. It stayed in place. Stephanie breathed a sigh of relief. As she turned to head back up the stairs, she looked up to see her face was at the level of Chance's crotch. He was standing there on the steps naked and aroused. "Come back to bed." Was all he said as he took Stephanie's hand. Stephanie breathed a deep excited breath; she wanted this even though she knew it was wrong.

~~~~~~

Hillary and Joe headed for the stable. When Joe brought out the horses, Hillary just took two steps back. She shook her head and laughed.

"And what my dear, do you expect me to do with that?" She asked

"You said you wanted to go to the ghost town." Joe responded.

"Yes, I did."

"Well, welcome to your transport."

"I don't know how to ride that. I am not into horses, although eating at a few places in the city, I may have had one of his ancestors for dinner." She laughed.

"That was not only vulgar, but disgusting."

"Hey, you eat in New York City at a couple of the questionable places and tell me what you think you are getting. Go on, just do it." She replied.

"No thanks, I think I'll pass. Look, it is this or nothing, the vehicles cannot make it back there. If you want to go, it is by horse."

"Ok, show me how." Hillary said as she climbed on the horse with Joe's help. "Look here horse, you be gentle

with me, no throwing me off or trampling me when you do.
Thank you for letting me sit on you."

Joe laughed at her, as he mounted his horse and
trotted up beside. He reached over, put the reigns of her
horse into her hands, and motioned for her to move. They
moved out slowly at first, but gained speed as they went
along. Hillary bounced around like a crazy person. She
actually looked as if she was having fun, but in an insane
way. It took twice as long as it should have but they finally
made it to the ghost town.

Joe dismounted and walked up to her. "So, are you
coming down?" He asked.

"Not unless you can get a doctor out here and
surgically remove me from this saddle." She said as she
laughed.

"Well at least you have kept your sense of humor."

They tied the horses and walked down to the center
of town. The wind was blowing, like a storm might set in
later. Brush blew past them and Hillary saw her first

tumble weed. Joe pointed down the street to where the house was. He tried his best to keep Hillary focused, but she was like a child on the loose. There were too many new sights and sounds to distract her.

"So, this is it?" Hillary asked as she walked up on the porch.

"Yeah, just be careful going inside; remember Stephanie went through the living room floor. If you stay to the edge you will be safe."

"Ok, I'll be careful. Just stay close to me. This place gives me the creeps. I keep expecting to see the ghost popping up."

They walked through the living room and Hillary was into everything. She was just too curious. As she made her way to the kitchen, she looked at the iron range stove in the front corner of the room. It was old and covered in rust and had charred-on grease. She made a disgusting face and then moved straight over to the wallpaper just as Stephanie had predicted. As she played with it, it flipped out freely and curled. Just then she saw the writing starting in the corner.

"What is this? Someone scribbled a message on the back." Hillary spoke not knowing what she had found.

"It's old and really faint but it's from Stephanie. She left us a note. She knew you would come looking at the house." Joe shouted.

Hillary's eyes began to water; she knew she was for a time safe. She breathed a sigh of relief and hugged Joe. He pulled the paper free and tore off the piece that was written on and handed it to Hillary.

"I believe this is yours. Hell-of-a souvenir huh?" He said.

"Yes, it is, and one of the best gifts I have ever gotten."

"So, what do we do now?" Joe asked.

"I don't know, just keep watching for clues I guess and pray she comes home soon."

"At least we know she is Ok and looking for a way back to us." Hillary responded, turning her head away to hide the tears that had begun to run down her face.

Chapter Thirteen: Search for the Truth

Stephanie grew more anxious with each hour she spent in the past. She had to find a way back to her time. She just needed a clue to what happened to the original Stephanie. Whether she was dead or not, the ghost version of Chance believed her dead and reincarnated. The living version seemed to accept Stephanie as the original version. Did he not know or remember? Stephanie couldn't wrap her head around it all. All she did know, was that she was giving herself a headache thinking about it.

Chance lay sleeping next to her on the bed. His naked body was bathed in the moonlight from the bedside window. Stephanie ran it all through her mind how Chance had taken her, again and again throughout the night. Her body still ached from the intensity of the sex. Now Stephanie watched Chance cautiously to make sure he was asleep. When she was sure, Stephanie slid herself out from under Chance's arm, and slipped on some clean clothes.

There had to be some clue left when the original Stephanie disappeared. She moved about the house in stealth mode, opening drawers and cabinets hoping to find anything. Just about the time she was ready to abandon the search, she saw the leather-bound book sticking from under the corner of the couch. She had not seen it before, but it was so obvious to her now.

Pulling it out, she nervously flipped through the pages. It was the other Stephanie's diary. Not knowing how much time she had, Stephanie read quickly, jumping from date to date. With every turn of a page, she glanced up to see if Chance had appeared on the stairs. Her luck held out as she raced to the back of the book. The original Stephanie had planned to escape from Chance, who had started to try to control her every move. Chance was jealous and feared of an affair that never happened. They had fought constantly, but it was all unfounded. The original Stephanie planned to stage an accident, so she would be taken to the doctor who had planned to help her win her freedom.

Stephanie closed the book and put it back safely where it had been hidden. She now knew she was in trouble. She would have to go, and go soon. Just as soon as Chance was up and preparing to go to work, Stephanie prepared herself to go as well. If answers were to be found, the doctor would probably have some.

Stephanie roamed the street of the town scanning every window and alleyway, to see if there was any sign that said doctor or something similar on it. The town was not too large; the sign had to be visible. On the last alley she crossed, she saw what she was looking for, a sign that read Dr. Baker.

Stephanie walked down the side street and started up the stairs that led to the second-floor doorway. She nervously glanced over her shoulder the whole time, looking like someone who was committing a crime. After reading the diary, she was scared of Chance.

At the top of the steps she knocked quietly on the door. For a moment there was nothing, then it slowly opened to reveal a very attractive and much younger man than Stephanie had anticipated, Dr. Baker.

Stephanie looked him up and down before speaking "Dr. Baker?" She asked.

"What are you doing here? I thought you were gone for good." He responded.

"Wow, this is going to take some explaining. I'm not who you think I am." Stephanie insisted.

"Yes, I see, you are not her. You just look exactly like her. But then again, if you were her, you would probably be dead, wouldn't you?" Dr. Baker said in a shaky voice.

"You were supposed to help her escape."

"How do you know that?" He asked.

"I found Stephanie's diary, and she was headed to you for help and a way out."

"She did, and she would have been fine, if Chance did not figure it all out. He followed Stephanie here, and as soon as I sent her off to a place to hide, Chance stopped her just outside of town. He captured Stephanie, and took her back to the barn where he worked, and it was there I am sure he killed her." The Doctor said, bracing himself as he sat down in his chair.

"Stephanie is dead and chance killed her. Now what do I do?" Stephanie mumbled out loud.

"It is obvious Chance is trying to cover up what he did by replacing the other Stephanie with you. No one would know of her death. I'd say that you have only one recourse. Turn the tables on him. Don't let him control the situation. He thinks he has all the cards since he is controlling everything and you. Don't let him."

"You're right. He trapped me into coming. He made sure I didn't know who I was, or what I was doing.

Now I am aware and it's time to fight back. Thank you for all your help. I have an idea what I have to do."

"If you need anything, just come back here and I will do what I can. Maybe, I will be able to do better by you than I did by the other Stephanie."

The door opened and Stephanie ran down the steps and rounded the corner just as Chance was coming into view. Stephanie drew a deep breath. She had never fought anyone for anything before, but to save her own life, she would fight.

She crossed the street staring Chance right in the face. Stephanie did not even flinch as she was within striking distance. She stayed strong and faked a smile.

"Where were you?" Chance asked.

"I was feeling really good today and decided to get some air and walk around a bit."

"I was scared when I woke up and you were gone. I thought you were ill again and went to the doctor without me."

"Nope, no need for a doctor. I seem to be healing really well on my own." Stephanie lied.

"I'm going to be late for work. Do you want me to go home and get you settled before I leave?"

"No, I think I will go with you. I am enjoying being out. I could help you out with your work. Maybe help you clean out the barn." Stephanie's voice became very sinister.

"You really don't have to." Chance said nervously.

"It's the least I could do, for all you have done for me."

The two walked in silence, all the way through town. Stephanie held her tongue as her anger grew. Chance was aware something was wrong, but he had no idea the tables were turning on him.

They mounted their horses and set off for the ranch. As they rode, Stephanie recognized a lot of the surroundings, from her rides to and from the ghost town in the future. Her mind drifted to Joe and how much she missed him. As her mind cleared, Stephanie thought of the time she had spent in Chance's bed and how she wished it had been Joe instead. Her memories of being the other Stephanie had almost completely faded. She thought about the sex they had and wondered if she went along with it because her conscious was somehow linked to the other Stephanie at the time. She felt guilty, regardless of who was in control when Chance was on top of her.

They came up on the barn quickly. As Stephanie looked around, she saw the original Ballin family house and the barn which in the future was gone. Where there would one day be a flower garden, there was now a building. She wished in her heart she could just blink and open her eyes and see the garden again. She just wanted to see Miss Elizabeth and Miss Mary there to greet her. Instead, she was over a hundred years away from them.

Chance went about his duties, as Stephanie walked into the barn. She surveyed the place. From every wall to roof beam, she diagramed the place in her mind. She was drawing up a war strategy. This was one war she did not plan to lose. As she moved about, she scanned the floor. If Stephanie had been killed there, then there had to be a sign of murder, or some evidence of what happened.

As Stephanie walked up to the back wall, she saw it, a pitchfork. It was hanging on the wall in plain sight. She ran her finger over the sharp points and then looked hard at the tips. There was blood on the ground below. Someone had wiped the fork clean but did not think about what had dripped before.

The other Stephanie was dead, but there was no sign of her being buried. The idea of what had happened there, ran chills down Stephanie's spine. She didn't want to end up like that. She had to find a way to turn the tables on Chance. Stephanie leaned against the wall laying her head back in deep thought. She didn't notice she was being watched, or that an eerie blue light was forming, just steps away from her. She was not alone.

Chapter Fourteen: Ghost from the Past Arise

Hillary and Joe had only been back from the ghost town a few minutes when the call came. It was the Ballin sisters. Their call was almost unintelligible. As soon as one sister would stop screaming, the other would start up and most times they were talking over each other so much you could not make out a word. Joe took the phone and told them to calm down and he and Hillary would be there immediately.

By the time they had reached the all too familiar front porch, Miss Mary ran out screaming, "She's here. Come quickly." Hillary and Joe looked at each other and ran for the garden. They both hoped that Stephanie had returned but in their hearts they both wondered if it could be that easy.

When they rounded the corner, they saw her. The beautiful young blond woman, dressed in western clothing, and looking so familiar to them. As Hillary's eyes met the woman's, she was overcome with emotions. Her heart was being ripped from the inside out. Joe tried to be strong and walked towards the blue light which was slowly turning more human in appearance.

"Are you Stephanie?" Joe asked.

"Yes, I'm Stephanie, just not your Stephanie. She is in the past as we speak, living a life that was mine. A life that was stolen from me."

Hillary drew a long hard breath and opened her mouth. "You're not her. She's still OK right?" She demanded.

"Yes, she is Ok, just getting ready to fight for her life. She knows the truth now. I have been watching her. I wasn't able to help her in the beginning. When she was wearing the ring, we were trapped together. Her body, and my memories were one. She figured it out though. As soon as she took off the ring, she got stronger and took over. She freed me without even knowing it"

Stephanie took full form mustering all the energy she could from her surroundings. She walked about the garden as she spoke, looking at the flowers the sisters had grown. She turned to them and smiled. After so much pain and death, this place had become a joy.

"I like what you have done here. For too long, I just thought of this as a place of murder. It was where I was in love once. A place where I fought with the man, I chose to spend my life with. It is where he took my life. I was buried just over there. Wasn't much of a burial, no one knew…just Chance. He hid it all really well."

"I am so sorry this happened to you." Hillary walked up to her as to extend her hand. "I guess that was stupid, you are a ghost. I can't touch you, can I?"

"Not so stupid, it was actually quite nice of you, to care for me like that. I see why Stephanie loves you so much. ...Why she loves all of you so much. I wish I had had that in life. I guess it just wasn't in the cards I was dealt. Maybe If I had family, I would still be alive."

"What about our Stephanie? Will she die?" Miss Elizabeth could not restrain herself any longer.

"No, she doesn't have to. I will protect her. She wants to come home. I have left her a few clues along the way to let her know what is happening and to be ready. I left her my journal, so she would know what happened and where to go to get answers. I want her to live, to have the life I was robbed of."

Hillary walked closer to her and smiled. "If I could hug you I would."

"You can, if you want, I can draw enough energy from my surroundings to become solid for a short time. It doesn't last long at all, and I can only do it a few times in my existence. But for you, I would."

Stephanie turned around in a circle, and her body began to glow a deep blue color. As she turned, the area all around her lit up with her light. A gentle wind started to blow through the flowers. As the wind blew harder, particles of light lifted up from the ground and swirled around her, absorbing into her body. She was becoming more solid by the minute.

As the wind died down, she turned to Hillary and reached out to her, and she took her hand. Hillary wrapped her arms around this Stephanie, just as she had done with her own. Their embrace felt like it lasted a lifetime. For Hillary it was what she needed, to renew her faith in the impossible. She knew her Stephanie could be saved.

"Thank-you ... for this moment of happiness. I have never wanted to become solid ever in all these years. It was very much worth it. Hillary, I need your help. The reason I came here is to ask for something. In order for Stephanie to get back here, I need something familiar to her that she can lock onto. Something to anchor her to this time."

"You mean like an object or possession?" Hillary asked.

"Yes, I am going to take it back to her, and when she holds it in her hands, she will be transported back here. Well, with a little help from me. I have to give her a little shove."

Hillary reached around her neck and released the clasp on the necklace she was wearing. As it slid off her shirt and into her hand, she held it out to Stephanie. Looking at it one last time, she allowed her to take it. Her face beamed with a smile.

"She gave me that years ago. It was her grandmother's. I have always treasured it. She said as long as I had it, it proved we were family. Tell her I want it back. It means more to me than anyone could ever know."

"I understand and I will guard it until I give it to her. I have to go now; Stephanie needs me and I don't know how much longer I can hold this form. Thank-you all. Oh, if you could, when all this is done and I can find my peace, could someone please have my body buried in a proper place. And a marker would be nice. I'd really like that a lot."

Stephanie smiled and the light returned around her as she started to become transparent. She waved good-bye to them all as the winds swirled a circle around her body. Engulfed totally in the light, she faded from view. The only evidence of her existence was a leaf cascading to the ground.

Hillary turned back to Joe. "I think all hell is about to break loose in the old west."

"Yeah, and now Chance has two versions of Stephanie after him. I'm not sure I would want to be in his shoes." Joe said as he exhaled.

"You two come on inside, I think we are going to have a long night." Miss Elizabeth spoke in a soft voice which was so unlike her.

"Yes Sister. This is a time for us to stick together. That's what families do for each other.

Hillary walked up behind Miss Elizabeth and put her arm around her and they walked inside together.

Chapter Fifteen: Joining Forces

Stephanie knew she was being watched. She was almost scared to open her eyes. Something didn't feel right. She breathed heavier and was almost scared to feel the temperature of the barn lowering. She felt the hair on the back of her neck standing up. She knew she just couldn't stand there, she had to do something. Slowly she opened her right eye just enough to see into the room, but not be obvious. Then she saw the blue glow.

Instantly, she popped open both her eyes and saw the room light up. The light was brilliant and blinding. Stephanie threw her arm up to block the light. It was at that point the light dimmed and formed a ball bouncing all around before settling just a few feet in front of her. The ball grew and took shape. Stephanie remembered Chance's ghost taking shape, it was all too familiar. She was almost scared; she knew what happened last time. And then she thought, something was different about this.

"Alright, who are you and what do you want from me?" Stephanie asked.

"Nothing." A static sounding voice came from the form.

"Well, being the last time, I saw something like this, I was dragged through time by ghost so I could be a sex toy for his younger living self, you have to understand my fear." She snapped.

"I'm not here to hurt you. I am here to help. What's a sex toy?"

"Never mind."

The light took form and shaped itself into the familiar form Stephanie recognized from the pictures at Mona's ranch. Stephanie studied her and walked around as the glow disappeared from the room. She looked her up and down. The resemblance the two had to each other was unreal. If the ghostly Stephanie had different hair, they would have been virtually identical.

"So, he really did kill you. I was sure of it when I found the pitch fork, but I just didn't want to believe it to be true." Stephanie said with a sad quivering voice.

"Yes, and I fear eventually the same might happen to you."

"I thought that too, I just don't understand something."

"What?"

"Why doesn't he know he killed you? Does he remember?" Stephanie asked.

"Did you remember who you were at first, when you were ripped backwards through time and placed here?" The ghost asked.

"No, my memory was screwed with, and until I got rid of the ring, I was not able to remember anything."

"Exactly, his memory has been tampered with too. His ghost probably put you both into a situation where you would just pick up like nothing was wrong. Trouble is, the issues from my past with him, would eventually show light again, and the whole thing would be destined to play out just as before." The ghost trailed off as she looked toward the pitch fork.

"What can I do? I am trapped here in the past waiting for whatever to happen. Even if I could get away, I don't know how to get home again to my time. And what is to stop the ghost from dragging me back here and doing this all over again." Stephanie said, becoming frustrated.

"It's simple really; we change the rules of the game and rewrite the story a bit. Where is the ring?"

"It's in my pocket. I have had it there ever since I took it off."

"Then we need to make sure it never makes its way back to where ever you found it."

"I found it in the cellar of the house. I was fool enough to pick it up and put it on." Stephanie replied.

"And that is how the ghost came for you. He used the ring like a beacon. When this is over, take the ring back to the future with you and get rid of it. If it never ends up in the cellar, this loop is broken."

"Ok, that much is solved, but I have to live long enough to get back to the future. Oh, and there is an interesting point. How the hell do I time travel back to where I am supposed to be?" Stephanie was becoming agitated.

"I already took care of that. I've been to your time. I saw your friends and explained to them what is going on, and that I will help you. Hillary loaned me something you gave her. We are going to use it as an anchor, when the time is right to send you back. Just like the ring was used to bring you here, her locket should drag you right back to her, with a little help from me." The ghost explained.

"What do we have to do to make that happen?" Stephanie asked.

"We have to change the past. Just a little bit. Not in a way that would make any difference or change your existence, but just right a wrong and get the same outcome."

Stephanie shook her head. She was getting a headache, but she agreed to go along with the ghost's plan. It was only a minute from the time the two had stopped talking, that Chance came walking towards the barn. Stephanie ran over to meet him at the door, giving time for the ghost to orb out of view. Chance was still playing his part and Stephanie did her best to fake her sincerity. If the plan was going to work, Stephanie was going to have to be the devoted lover to the last minute. To save her life, Stephanie was willing to do anything. She just wanted out of the old west.

"Aren't you getting tired of hanging out in this old barn. It's a sunny day, get out and get some air." Chance whispered in her ear, as he began to kiss down Stephanie's neck.

Stephanie laughed. "I kind of like it here. It's peaceful and quiet. I can think without interruption."

"You are always in your head thinking, dreaming, you should be out in the real world with the rest of us."

"There is nothing wrong with a vivid imagination. Besides, without dreams we would have no ambition or drive." Stephanie insisted.

"Ok already, you win. For once, I will let you have your way."

Stephanie unbuttoned her shirt as she walked to the door of the barn and looked out at the brilliant colors of the day. The sky was filled with blue and the land around blended into the horizon making the whole scene look like an oil painting. She found it beautiful. For a moment she was taken in by her surroundings, but she knew there was death and danger hiding behind all this beauty.

Chance walked up behind her and reached through Stephanie's arms and wrapped around her chest. For a moment Stephanie wondered how this man, who had been so loving to her, could be the same man who killed the other Stephanie. She took a deep breath and let it out slowly. She did not want to give herself away.

"Why don't we go home and have lunch, and then later this evening come back and watch the sun go down." Chance said as he kissed Stephanie's neck.

"I'd like that, it sounds romantic. I'd like the time out of the house."

Chance went off to do a couple of things before they went home and Stephanie walked back to the pitchfork. She stared at it trying to understand how someone could take another person's life. She didn't know if she was capable.

"I heard what Chance said." The ghost voice came out of nowhere.

"When do we change history?" Stephanie asked.

"Tonight."

"I don't know if I can do this. I know it has to happen."

"Just get him here, and I'll do the rest." The ghost explained.

"What'll happen to you in the end? Are you going to be stuck here?" Stephanie asked.

"I don't know. I would like to think that in finding justice, I can go to the other side."

"You are stuck here because you have unfinished business?"

"Yes, it happens that way. Ghosts who have messages they have to pass, or things they have to accomplish, stay here for a while until they can do whatever needs to be done. And sometimes, if you die in a violent way, it takes a while to be released. And one way to get it over with is to resolve the conflict.

There are no set rules for how long you are here in limbo, or if you ever crossover at all. It is just a sad and often lonely existence at times. I mean, just imagine being able to see everything you had in life, the people, the places and what meant the most to you, and not be able to interact with what was your life. And then deal with the idea someone took it all from you in a jealous rage." Anger flowed through the ghost's voice.

"I am so sorry this happened to you." Stephanie dropped her head in sadness. The words of the ghost resonated in her brain. There was so much anger and hurt. This was once a woman who would have been just like her. They were so similar in feelings and appearance. Stephanie could not comprehend how someone such as herself could travel through so much pain to want to enact revenge on another. But she also knew that to survive, you do anything you have to.

"Be here tonight, and follow my lead when I am ready for you." The ghost insisted.

"I don't understand how this will work. You are a ghost, what can you do to save me from Chance." Stephanie questioned her.

"As I told Hillary, when I visited the future, I can become solid for a brief time. I will be just as you are. It won't last long, maybe just a few minutes. But just a few minutes, should be enough for what I have in mind. It worked in the future, that is how I got the locket. When the time is right, I will trade places with you. You will need to get outside the barn quickly. When I am done, I will come to you, and with the locket I will help you go home. Just do whatever I tell you to."

"I understand. You better get out of here before Chance comes back."

Stephanie turned around to find Chance looking in the door. His expression had changed, Chance looked angry. He stormed into the barn looking around as if someone had been there.

"Who were you talking to?" Chance demanded to know.

"No one, I am here alone." Stephanie insisted.

"I heard you talking to someone." Chance raised his voice grabbing Stephanie by the arms.

"There was no other living person in this barn. I swear, I am telling you the truth." Stephanie screamed as she pulled free from Chances grip. She rubbed her arms which were still in intense pain. "If you don't believe me look around."

"Then who were you talking to?"

"I was just talking to myself. Thinking out loud." Stephanie said sarcastically.

Chance turned to her and before Stephanie could block it, a fist flew upside her head. Stephanie fell to the ground. As she reached for her mouth Stephanie knew that blood was all over her face. She tried to stand up but couldn't. She saw Chance's mouth moving, but couldn't hear anything for the loud ringing in her ears.

It had happened. It was at this point, Stephanie understood how you could harm another. She didn't want to die. No one had ever laid a hand on her before. Now she knew why she had to defend herself. She felt the ghost's pain along with hers. Sadly, the other Stephanie didn't have a chance to get back up again.

"Stephanie…can you hear me. Look at me, let me know you are in there." Chance pleaded with her.

"I am fine." Stephanie lied.

"Why do you do things like that? You know I have a temper and when you make me angry, I sometimes can't control it. Come on, let's get you cleaned up and I'll take you home and make you dinner."

Stephanie stood up and locked her body into place, as Chance cleaned her face off. The bleeding had stopped and the ringing had left Stephanie's ears, but the pain and disgust weren't going away soon. As they walked out of the barn, Stephanie stared at Chance. Her thoughts were of revenge not just for herself but for the ghost who suffered so much more than she had.

Chapter Sixteen: Revenge Comes in Many Forms

As Stephanie rode back to the house with Chance, her guard was up. She wasn't going to take any risks. She didn't want a pitch fork ending up in her back. Her mind raced all over the place. The pain made her head ache every time the horse would move. She wanted so badly to run to Hillary and get comfort. She was her protector, friend and family all rolled into one. She could only imagine what Hillary was thinking at the time with all that had happened.

Stephanie was sure of one thing though, she had to be strong. If she was to get home again, this fight was far from over. As they rode, Chance looked at her over and over again. His facial expression was a cross between a homicidal maniac and a concerned lover. As Stephanie watched him, Chance's expression changed continuously, as if he were arguing with himself. Chance was out of control and Stephanie knew it. If his ghost wiped his memory, then Chance was reverting.

The whole idea sent a chill down Stephanie's spine. She could handle the Chance that had been reprogrammed, but she wasn't ready to tangle with the murderer within. Stephanie was going to act as if everything was fine and not enrage Chance. They arrived home and Stephanie made the first move to smooth the waters.

"What are you making me for dinner?" Stephanie asked.

"Anything you want. Look, I am really sorry you got hurt."

"Don't...I am fine. Let's put it behind us. I'm hungry and excited about going to the barn to see the sunset." Stephanie leaned in and hugged him while looking to the ceiling and squinting her eyes in disgust.

"Why don't you go clean up and wash off any blood I missed." Chance insisted handing her a basin of water.

Stephanie headed upstairs and placed the basin on the dresser. She looked into the mirror. The side of her face was swollen, yet she thought she looked better than she felt. She shook her head and thought to herself, 'I won't be this stupid again, ever.' She put a cloth into the water and rung it out. As she ran it down the swelling in her cheek, the raw burning feeling made her angry. She puffed up her cheeks and blew the air out. It hurt more than she was ready for, but she had to wipe the blood off.

Stephanie pulled off her shirt, which had blood all around the collar near the front. She folded it and laid it on the bed. She felt hot and sticky from the day. The heat had gotten to her on the way home. She took off the rest of her clothes and used the cloth to wipe away the sweat. As she was bending over to wipe off her legs, Chance entered from behind.

"I can help you with that if you want." He offered as his mouth hung open.

"I was just cleaning up quickly for dinner. I'm fine." Stephanie replied trying to not allow Chance the opportunity to touch her naked body.

"No, let me help you, you're getting red in the face. Just stand up and I will do it for you."

Stephanie stood back up, as Chance wrung out the cloth again. He fell to his knees and began to run the cloth over Stephanie's right leg. As he wiped, Chance stared intently at Stephanie's naked body. He was aroused. His mouth filled with saliva; he was hungry for Stephanie's body. As he moved around and wiped Stephanie's backside, Chance touched himself and tried to free his tightened jeans. He loved looking at Stephanie naked, but he loved it more when he was in control and taking Stephanie aggressively. And now, he wanted to dominate her more than ever. He wanted to aggressively make Stephanie submit to his manhood, no matter how much it hurt her.

Stephanie quivered as the cloth ran down her crack. Fear possessed her; she didn't want this to be a reoccurrence of the last couple of days in the bedroom. She had been turned on at the time, by Chance's animalistic aggressive sex. But the fascination had been replaced by a disgusting hatred. Stephanie knew she had to play her part but she was not prepared to have Chance inside her again.

As Chance continued to wipe, there was no doubting what was on his mind as his manhood hung out of the buttons of his jeans. He smiled up at Stephanie. His expression told of his hunger. He was ready to explode. Stephanie didn't know what to do. She had to stop this from happening. As she was about to open her mouth and offer anything that might save her, her savior came in a wave of smoke from the kitchen.

"Oh god the food is burning." Chance moaned as he jumped to his feet and headed down the stairs.

Stephanie was thankful for the reprieve. She had been spared. She quickly looked for clothes and got dressed. She had to get downstairs, before Chance came back and caught her naked again. She moved more quickly than she ever had in her life. Stephanie was dressed and down the stairs before Chance could get the stove under control.

"Aww…. you got dressed." Chance commented as he saw Stephanie.

"I wanted to make sure you didn't burn the place down."

"I had another fire in mind upstairs in the bedroom."

"I bet you did." Stephanie mumbled as she turned away.

"What, I couldn't hear you?" Chance questioned.

"Oh nothing, I was just agreeing with you."

"Well, the food isn't too burned. It should be ready in a minute."

Stephanie went about setting the table and preparing to eat. She knew the sooner they got back to the barn, the better. As she watched chance get the food together, she thought about what had happened upstairs. She couldn't understand how a man who was beating her earlier, had become so sexually aroused. It was all so sick to her. She could only guess it was about control and Chance's need for satisfaction. Stephanie was sure at this point she did not want to be beaten by Chance, or give in to his sex drive ever again.

Mullins

Chapter Seventeen: Revenge of the Dead

Hillary sat quietly. As anyone who knew her would tell you, this was not good. She was scared and she never got scared. Everything that had happened was out of her realm of understanding. She liked being in control and in this situation, there was no one in control of what happened to Stephanie except a ghost from the past and his former living self.

"I hate waiting. I just want this over with." Hillary moaned.

"It will be over with soon enough. It just has to happen when the time is right in the past. Have a little faith in Stephanie." Joe tried to reassure her.

"Oh, I have faith in Stephanie, but when you throw in two ghosts and a murderer, then I get a little uneasy. I miss her so much. I am so used to seeing her every day, and then to have her ripped away from me. I just thought I was stronger than this."

"You are doing great. I am so proud of you for holding up the way you have."

"I guess there is one bright point in all of this." Hillary added. "I usually hate every man Stephanie ever introduces me to. You, I don't hate so much."

Joe laughed out loud. "Thanks, I guess."

"You're welcome and it was a very big compliment. I think you are just wonderful, and I am glad to think of you as a friend. I don't have a lot of friends and I choose the ones I let in very carefully. I hope if things go well with you and Stephanie that you will be a part of our family."

"I'd like that very much." Joe looked down away from Hillary so she couldn't see the tears in his eyes. He knew, he wanted Stephanie more than anything.

Miss Elizabeth and Miss Mary returned from the kitchen where they had been starting dinner. The group had agreed they would stay together until it was over. They sat with Hillary and Joe, no one knowing what they should be doing, or if they had to prepare. It was a waiting game now.

~~~~~~

As Chance and Stephanie finished dinner, she went about cleaning up. Just as she washed the last dish, Chance came up behind Stephanie and wrapped his arms around her. Stephanie almost flinched, but instead leaned back into him. She had to make Chance believe she was the loving partner. Even though inside it turned her stomach.

Chance held on tighter to her and lowered his arms down to Stephanie's waist. With a quick motion, he reached down and unbuttoned Stephanie's pants allowing them to fall to the floor. Chance rubbed himself up and down Stephanie's backside leaving nothing to the imagination. He was determined to have what he had desired all day. As he slowly slid off Stephanie's underwear, he was like a demon attacking.

Stephanie turned around and pulled him in tight. Their lips met, and Chance kissed her hard, forcing their mouths tightly together. Slowly he worked his way down Stephanie's neck. Chance's rough unshaven face left burn marks wherever he kissed. As he fell to his knees, he was at eye level with Stephanie's exposed waist.

As Chance was about to put his mouth between Stephanie's legs, Stephanie backed off. Chance just fell back with a questioning look on his face. He couldn't imagine why Stephanie stopped. Chance was a man on fire and he wanted what he came for.

"What's wrong? Why did you stop? I thought you wanted me." Chance questioned her.

"I do want you. I have been looking forward to being with you all day. Just not here or now. I want to go to the barn and have our romantic night. And then after we are alone there, I want to give you everything you deserve." Stephanie said, as she pulled Chance up by his collar and forced her lips on him.

"Oh, I get it, you want a change of pace, the excitement of something new. I like that. Let's get going, the sooner we get there the sooner we can continue." Chance said wiping the wetness from his mouth.

As they prepared to leave, Chance stayed glued to Stephanie. He was like a wild animal stalking his kill. Stephanie was a little scared by the obsessed look in Chance's eyes. She quickly pulled together a blanket and candles that they would need in the barn. Then they were off.

They rode hard on the way there. Every time Stephanie would slow down, Chance would encourage her to speed up. Stephanie was worried. She had seen no sign of the ghost since earlier. If she did not show up, what would happen? Stephanie did not want to die that night, and not in the barn like her predecessor.

As they arrived at the barn, the last of the ranch hands were leaving for the night. It gave Stephanie a few minutes to look around, before Chance was all over her. She walked around to the rear of the building and still saw no sign of the ghost. Now she was really nervous and began to pace. She had no desire to have Chance all over her.

Just as total fear ran through her body the familiar blue light appeared. Stephanie turned towards it and breathed a deep sigh of relief. In seconds, she was looking face to face with the ghost.

"Where have you been, I was scared to death? Do you know how hard it is to keep his hands off of me? Not to mention other body parts." Stephanie blasted at her.

"I'm sorry. I had to gather my energy. To do what we have to tonight, I am going to have to become solid again. It takes a lot of time to gather that much energy."

"So how is this going to work? What do I do?" Stephanie asked.

"Seduce him. Get him naked and tie him up. Then I take over."

"What are you going to do?"

"I'm going to give him a dose of his own medicine. I will let you know when the time is right." The ghost grinned and walked away.

Chance came into the barn as soon as he knew they were alone. He called for Stephanie and started to lay the blanket out on the hay that covered the floor. Stephanie walked around the corner looking calm. She had found her confidence.

"Now, where were we?" Chance asked her as Stephanie fell to her knees on the blanket.

"I think you were telling me that you like trying something new." Stephanie teased him.

"Yes, I really want that." Chance breathed heavy as he pulled off his shirt and started tugging at his boots.

Stephanie watched him, as he anxiously shed his clothes. A smile came across Stephanie's lips, as she imagined Chances face when she and the ghost switched places. Stephanie ran the whole scenario through her brain. Stephanie had switched sides; she was no longer the victim. She was now the predator. She stared a Chance in all his nakedness. It pleased her, to be in control finally. She had been a victim long enough.

"What's that look mean?" Chance said in an uneasy voice.

"Oh nothing, I'm just enjoying the situation. I like having you here naked. By the looks of it, you are enjoying it too." Stephanie said staring at him intently.

Stephanie moved around, and from under the blanket she pulled out the rope she had brought with her.

She came closer to Chance and leaned down over him. "Don't worry, I won't hurt you much." Stephanie whispered in his ear. "...Unless you want me to."

She reached down and took Chance's hand in hers, and pulled it up, then seductively wrapped the rope around it. She then pulled Chance's other hand behind his back and tied the two together. As Stephanie pulled tighter, she leaned back into Chance's ear and she said, "Bet you thought I was harmless. I'm not hurting you, am I?" Chance shook his head no. The rope stimulated him more than he had ever known.

Stephanie kneeled between Chance's legs, and slowly crisscrossed the rope around his entire body. Her final move was to tie Chance's legs behind him so that he was in a bound sitting position. Chance looked up at Stephanie. His mind was racing in all different directions wondering what Stephanie would do next. He had never been this turned on before.

Stephanie stood up and moved back a couple of steps and looked at what she had done. She was impressed that she was able to recreate what she had seen on the internet one time. Stephanie was never in to bondage, but the knowledge did come in handy.

"Well, don't just keep me waiting. What are you going to do?" Chance asked her.

"Oh, there are so many things I would love to do. Just not with you. You have already had as much of me as you will ever have."

"What do you mean, you just can't tie me up and get me going like this and walk away." Chance growled at her. "What's going on, what's with the blue light. Cut me loose now!"

"Don't worry; I am going to leave you in capable hands. I believe you remember my good friend Stephanie. You killed her. You might not remember too well that you did it. But then again maybe you do. You see I got my memory back some time ago. And I am guessing by your personality change, so did you."

Just as Stephanie was finishing her line, the ghost's light completely filled the room. Stephanie looked at the ghost, who was just taking solid form. The ghost looked back and they both exchanged smiles, as Stephanie walked over to the door. She turned around again, to take one last look at Chance.

"You know when I first got here and didn't really remember who I was, I didn't think you were all that bad. I almost enjoyed being with you. But when I remembered, and figured out what you are all about, I really got disgusted. I can't even imagine how you could take another person's life. Stephanie was innocent and you took away everything from her. Now you are going to learn what it feels like."

As Stephanie turned back to the door, the ghost followed her. "Wait for me outside." The ghost spoke in a low tone. Stephanie shook her head in agreement. She was ready for all this to end.

"Oh Chance…one last thing, you wanted to be screwed." Stephanie glared at him. "Now you are screwed." As Stephanie walked away from the closing door, she could hear Chance's blood chilling screams getting louder and louder.

Chapter Eighteen: Death Be Not Proud

Stephanie walked away from the door.   She tried to not hear the screaming, by clouding her head with thoughts, music, anything she could imagine. It did no good, she knew what was going on, and what was about to happen. As much as she tried to rationalize, that she had to allow this to happen to save her life, it didn't weigh in any easier on her conscious.

Inside the barn, the ghost hardly had to do anything to scare the hell out of Chance. As she walked circles around the barn, she took a little bit of satisfaction that her mere presence was enough to exact a small level of revenge. As she walked to the back wall, the ghost of Stephanie looked up and saw the pitchfork hanging there.

A grim reminder of the pain she suffered, and the trauma involved in the robbing of her life from her. Her anger grew as she reached up and took the instrument of murder in her hands.

As she looked down at the pitch fork and then over to Chance, it all flooded back, from her memories like a dam which had just broken. She was washed over with every memory she had suppressed since the day she died. Her eyes glazed over, as the memories played through. She and Chance had come there, the same way Stephanie had just done. They were supposed to have an evening together. Except the ending was much different, Chance flew into one of his wild jealous rages. He had accused Stephanie of being with another man. Stephanie swore it was not true, but Chance did not believe her. …And when Stephanie turned to walk away…blackness.

Chance had hit her on the back of the head. As she lay there unconscious, Chance ran her through several times with the pitchfork. Now, she knew exactly how she died. She turned to Chance.

"You killed me. You didn't even have the decency to face me when you did it. You knocked me out, and then took my life. All because you didn't believe what I told you. I never was with anyone but you." The ghost's echoed voice got louder and clearer.

"I was so sure you cheated on me." Chance cried out.

"There was no proof. Not one thing to lead you to believe that."

"I saw you with the doctor. You were there with him." Chance defended himself.

"I was with the doctor, because he was treating me for all the times you hurt me."

"He was trying to take you away from me."

"No, he was helping me plan an escape from you. Because he was sure one day you would kill me. Guess he was right. You took my life for no good reason at all. Not that there is ever a good reason to take a life. Now maybe it is time for me to return the favor." The ghost's eyes began to glow as her voice trailed off.

The ghost looked at the pitchfork and then at Chance. She just couldn't do it. She was no more capable, than the woman who had just walked out of the door. They might have been from two different times and possibly the reincarnation of the other, but neither was capable of taking a life. The ghost stabbed the pitchfork into the ground as she breathed a heavy breath.

"I knew you weren't woman enough to do it." Chance berated her. "You were always a weak pathetic cunt. It was easy to kill you. You were never woman enough for me anyway."

The ghost of Stephanie turned and walked back to him and kneeled down. "I was more woman, than you will ever know. And no, I am not woman enough to kill you right now. Not with my bare hands and surely not with a pitchfork. And definitely not when you were unconscious and defenseless. Only a coward would do that. But I am ghost enough to tip over this lantern and watch this place burn." Just then a sinister grin ran across her face. She was about to get justice and she knew it.

The ghost rocked the lantern back and forth with her hand. The whole time Chance began to sweat. Tears ran down Chance's face as the ghost stood up and kicked over the lamp. A final scream bellowed throughout the barn as the ghost became transparent again, turned and walked through the door.

Outside, Stephanie waited for her. "Is it over? Can we go now?" She asked.

"We can leave in a minute or two. I just want to make sure the fire does its job."

The flames spread quickly, and the barn was fully engulfed as the ghost reached into her pocket. She pulled out the piece of jewelry she had gotten from Hillary and handed it to Stephanie.

"Do you remember this?" The ghost asked.

"Yes, Hill loves it so much. How did you get her to part with it?"

"She loves you more. Now, it's time to go home. Focus on the love you have for Hillary and the reason you gave her this. Now remember how badly you want to be back with her and focus on where she is now."

The ghost moved close to Stephanie and engulfed her in the blue light. As she came closer, she put her arms around Stephanie. For a moment all was quiet and then everything around them started to change. Time began to speed up and as they watched their surroundings age, they went speeding toward the future.

The barn burned to the ground in a couple of seconds and then it was gone. Seasons came and went in the blink of an eye and the further they moved through time, the faster it happened. Buildings became aged, then fell and were removed. They were replaced with more modern constructions. The area around them changed from a field of grass, to crops growing, and then to grass again. Finally, the first signs of flowers occurred. Two young girls were planting all around them. Stephanie smiled; she knew who they were.

~~~~~~

A storm formed in the sky above the house. It grew so fast in intensity with lightning and thunder so much that the Ballin sisters became scared. These storms were not normal there, they hardly ever had rain and when the rain came many times it led to flash floods. They moved to the back door to get a better look at what was going on.

"This isn't good sister." Miss Mary commented.

"No sister. Something is coming for sure, and I don't mean just weather."

Hillary and Joe joined them and the group moved to the garden. The wind swirled and they felt the charge of electricity in the air. In the center of the garden a light began to form. It was a familiar thing at this point. The brilliant white ball grew and began to change to blue. Hillary looked over at Joe; she knew Stephanie was coming back.

As the light took shape it extended its range and a large portal formed. Both Stephanie and the ghost stepped out. Tears ran down Hillary's face as she moved towards Stephanie. She walked slowly at first and then galloped towards her.

"I'm home. Did you miss me?" Stephanie asked.

"More than you will ever know." Hillary replied.

Joe came from behind and joined them in their hug. Stephanie held on as long as she could. She was happy to be home. Then she turned to the ghost.

"What'll happen to you now? Where will you go?" Stephanie had to ask.

"I resolved my unfinished business. Now it is time for me to go."

"You will pass over into the light." Hillary asked.

"Yeah, something like that." The ghost smiled. "I'm ready to go now."

"When?" Stephanie asked.

"Right now. You can't see it, can you?" The ghost said pointing to the brilliant light only she could see.

"No, I can't see it, but go, you have been waiting so long for this. Just…one last thing, thank-you, if it wasn't for you, I would have never made it home again."

"It's Ok, I think we both got something out of this. I'll be watching out for you on the other side."

The ghost stepped through the light and was gone. The wind died down completely, and the storm was gone too. It was as if nothing ever happened. But in Stephanie's mind she knew it did happen and a lot of damage had been done. But there was a positive ending; she had found a new family.

"I hope everyone's hungry, we made dinner and it should be ready right now." Miss Mary said impressed with her timing.

Mullins

Afterwards

The days after the ordeal went fast, and before long, Stephanie was at the end of her planned vacation. She and Joe had become closer than ever. Stephanie couldn't deal with the idea of going back and facing her mundane life in the city. On the last night, Joe took Stephanie and Hillary into the desert to cook food outdoors and enjoy their last night together. As they sat watching the stars, Stephanie realized she had to make a decision.

"We all have to talk. This trip has been so much more than I ever planned."

"I'd say being ripped through time by a ghost, and rescued by your previous self as a ghost, was not on your itinerary." Hillary laughed hard.

"Yeah you could say that. But being here has been so much more. I like it here and I like all the people we have met. And Joe, I don't know how I could ever leave you." Stephanie took a deep breath realizing she had said it all out loud.

"Don't then. I will go back to the city with you." Joe responded.

"You wouldn't be happy there. You wouldn't last a day." Stephanie realized she was right before the words left her lips.

"Well at first, I didn't think you would last a day here. But you did."

"I was never that happy in the city. Coming here, and not being tied to computers and cell phones, has been wonderful. It's been more about the people here. The only thing that made my life in the city worth anything, was you Hillary. You are my family."

"And you are mine." She replied. "But I think I have a solution that will work for everyone."

"What's that?" Joe asked.

"I think Stephanie and I need to make a change. It is time to start life anew here. I love it here too. I don't want to go back to the boring life we left behind. Besides, I met this ranch hand that I am sure is going to make me so happy," Hillary laughed insanely.

"So, I guess it is settled then. We are home." Stephanie breathed a sigh of relief.

As Stephanie stood up, she walked out away from the others and surveyed the wide-open landscape. She rested her hands in her pockets and realized there was something she still had to do. She reached deep inside and found the last remnant of her ordeal. She pulled out her hand, and in it was the ring that reminded her so much of Chance. She looked at it for a second. There was nothing but sadness attached to it. Stephanie pulled back her hand, clinched a fist, and threw the ring as hard as she could into the desert night. It was gone now, and there was no longer any tie to the past.

She walked back to the others and looked down at her new family. She smiled and knew how lucky she was.

"Hillary, would you please take that damn safari hat off of Samantha?"

"Why? She likes it so much. Besides I would look stupid being the only one here wearing one." Hillary laughed as she hugged the cat, and smiled at Stephanie.

Daniel walked in the land of the dead. Now the dead want him back!

For Information About

From The Dead Of Night

The Book Series Visit
gwmullins.wixsite.com/books

About the Author

Thanks for choosing this book, if you enjoyed it, please leave positive feedback.

G.W. Mullins is an Author, Photographer, and Entrepreneur of Native American / Cherokee descent. He has been a published author for over 10 years. His writing has focused on the paranormal and Native American studies. Mullins has released several books on the history/stories/fables of the Native American Indians.

Among his books are the extremely successful *Star People, Sky Gods, And Other Tales Of The Native American Indians*, *The Native American Story Book - Stories Of The American Indians For Children Volumes 1-5*, *The Native American Cookbook*, and *Walking With Spirits Native American Myths, Legends, And Folklore Volumes 1 Thru 6*.

He has released the complete series from his Sci/fi Fantasy Series *From The Dead Of Night*, including the Best-Selling titles - *Daniel Is Waiting*, and *Daniel Returns*.

His most recent work includes the new series *Rise Of The Snow Queen* featuring *Book One The Polar Bear King*, and *Book Two The War Of The Witches*. He has also released *Messages from The Other Side* a nonfiction book about communication with the dead.

For further information, on his writing, visit G.W. Mullins' web site at *http://gwmullins.wix.com/books*.

Also Available From G.W. Mullins

Rise Of The Snow Queen Book Two The War Of The Witches

Daniel Awakens A Ghost Story Begins– From The Dead Of Night Prequel

Daniel Is Waiting A Ghost Story – From The Dead Of Night Book One

Daniel Returns A Ghost Story - From The Dead Of Night Book Two

Daniel's Fate A Ghost Story Ends - From The Dead Of Night Book Four

Rise Of The Snow Queen Book One The Polar Bear King

Messages From The Other Side Stories of the Dead, Their Communication, and Unfinished Business

Vengeance

Mysteries Of The Unseen World – Ghost, Hauntings and The Unexplained

Haunted America Stories Of Ghost, Hauntings And The Unexplained

Timeless – A Paranormal Romance Murder Mystery

Star People, Sky Gods, And Other Tales Of The Native American Indians

More Star People, Sky Gods, And Other Paranormal Tales Of The Native American Indians

Lost Tales Of The Native American Indians Vol 1

Walking With Spirits Native American Myths, Legends, And Folklore Volumes One Thru Six

The Native American Cookbook

Native American Cooking - An Indian Cookbook With Legends And Folklore

The Native American Story Book - Stories Of The American Indians For Children
Volumes One Thru Five

The Best Native American Stories For Children

Cherokee A Collection of American Indian Legends,
Stories And Fables

Creation Myths - Tales Of The Native American Indians

Strange Tales Of The Native American Indians

Spirit Quest - Stories Of The Native American Indians

Animal Tales Of The Native American Indians

Medicine Man - Shamanism, Natural Healing, Remedies
And Stories Of The Native American Indians

Native American Legends: Stories Of The Hopi Indians
Volumes One and Two

Totem Animals Of The Native Americans

The Best Native American Myths, Legends And Folklore
Volumes One Thru Three

Ghosts, Spirits And The Afterlife In Native American
Indian Mythology And Folklore

Origin Tales Of The Native American